In the Frame

Samantha Alexander lives in Lincolnshire with a
variety of animals including her thoroughbred
horse, Bunny, and a pet goose called Bertie. Her
schedule is almost as busy and exciting as her plots
– she writes a number of columns for newspapers
and magazines, is a teenage agony aunt for BBC
Radio Leeds and in her spare time she regularly
competes in dressage and showjumping.

Also by Samantha Alexander
and available from Macmillan

RIDERS

HOLLYWELL STABLES

RIDERS

5

In the Frame

SAMANTHA ALEXANDER

MACMILLAN CHILDREN'S BOOKS

First published 1997 by
Macmillan Children's Books
a division of Macmillan Publishers Ltd
25 Eccleston Place, London SW1W 9NF
and Basingstoke

Associated companies throughout the world

ISBN 0 330 34537 0

3 5 7 9 8 6 4 2

A CIP catalogue record for this book is available from the British Library.

Phototypeset by Intype London Ltd
Printed by Mackays of Chatham plc, Chatham, Kent

For Patrick.
In memory of a dear friend

Samantha Alexander and Macmillan Children's Books would like to thank *Horse and Pony* magazine for helping us by running a competition to find our cover girl, Sally Johnson. Look out for more about the **Riders** and **Hollywell Stables** series in *Horse and Pony* magazine and find out more about Samantha by reading her agony column in every issue.

Macmillan Children's Books would also like to thank Chris White; and David Burrows and all at Sandridgebury Stables, especially Toby and his owner Sylvie.

And finally thanks to Angela Clarke from Ride-Away in Sutton-on-Forest, Yorkshire for providing the riding clothes, hats and boots featured on the covers.

CHARACTERS

Alexandra Johnson Our heroine. 14 years old. Blonde, brown eyes. Ambitious, strong-willed and determined to become a top eventer. Owns Barney, a 14.2 hh dun with black points.

Ash Burgess Our hero. 19 years old. Blond hair, blue eyes, flashy smile. Very promising young eventer. He runs the livery stables for his parents. His star horse is Donavon, a 16.2 hh chestnut.

Zoe Jackson Alex's best friend. 15 years old. Sandy hair, freckles. Owns Lace, a 14.1 hh grey.

Camilla Davies Typical Pony Club high-flyer. 15 years old. Owns The Hawk, a 14.2 hh bay.

Judy Richards Ash's head groom and sometime girlfriend. 18 years old.

Eric Burgess Ash's uncle. Around 50 years old. His legs were paralysed in a riding accident. He has a basset hound called Daisy.

Look out for the definition-packed glossary of horsey terms at the back of the book.

CHAPTER ONE

"I'm useless, I've lost it. I can't ride to save my life."

"Poppycock." Eric, my mentor and trainer, banged his arm on his wheelchair in a fit of temper. "You're not hungry enough, that's all. You've lost the desire."

We were at a one-day event. I was sitting on an upturned bucket in floods of tears and my horse, Barney, was sulking because I'd pulled him up halfway round the cross-country course. I'd literally forgotten my way. I'd sat there in the middle of a grassy stretch not knowing which way to turn until someone had shouted from the railings and I'd pushed Barney on and jumped the water jump the wrong way round. The red flag should always be to your right and the white one to your left. I was instantly eliminated.

We'd travelled a hundred and twenty miles and I hadn't even completed the course. Barney was scowling at me and refused an apple core which he usually loves.

Eric Burgess, former *chef d'équipe* of the Olympic team, had made me a promise that in

1

a year's time I'd be competing at the National Championships.

"Everybody loses form." He passed me a plastic cup of stewed tea and ordered me to drink. "Look at some of the great tennis players, golfers, swimmers – everybody has off days. The secret to being a champion is to work out why and put it right."

I gulped down more tea and set about bandaging up Barney for the long trip home. Ash, my boyfriend, had been competing in a different class for novice horses with a brilliant mare called Dolly who was an ex-polo pony and could jump a five-foot gate from a standstill. The rosettes and trophy were in the horsebox cab. He now had a new sponsor, Sir Charles, who was ploughing money into eventing, and the two of them were scouring all the events for potential new horses. It was exciting and exhilarating. Horses kept turning up in the yard from all over the country. Ash even had to take on more staff. Sometimes, like now, I got just a teeny bit jealous. If I had a string of horses I might do better; I'd have more experience, more rides.

Eric was Ash's uncle and had been paralysed from the waist down after a riding accident. He would have gone berserk if he had heard me talking like that. Barney was 14.2, a dun Arab/Connemara cross with the guts and character of twenty thoroughbreds. I loved him to bits but he was a rogue to ride and he wasn't particularly flashy. Now Dolly, for instance, was perfect . . .

Ash stalked back to the horsebox, his gold-blond hair falling forward, his eyes bright with excitement. At nineteen he was one of the bright hopes for the future. Perhaps for the next Olympics. He had everything a top rider needed, from bags of natural talent to bucket loads of courage.

"I've found three more horses," he exclaimed, tapping Sir Charles' number into his mobile phone. "What's the matter with you? You've got a face like a rainy day."

Five hours later we pulled into the yard and unloaded the horses feeling stiff and tired and ready for a hot bath. We'd stopped at a Little Chef for steak and chips and I'd read *In the Saddle* cover to cover. There was an article all about Ian Jones, and William McNally-Smith's bad luck at the Olympics. "At least they'd walked the course properly." Ash changed into a lower gear as we struggled up a Derbyshire hill. "If you'd spent less time trying on new jodhpurs and more time looking at fences you'd probably have come first."

"All right, Mr Know-it-all, put a sock in it. Just wait till you make a mistake." I stuck my tongue out at him. "I'll never let you forget it."

"Alex Johnson, you're a bad loser but I love you to bits. Now where's that road map?"

*

We put the horses in their stables, changed the rugs and gave them a bran mash with sliced carrots and molasses. Barney had a special clip-on manger which hung over his door so he could eat and still see everything.

Reggie and Nigel, the two stable ducks, came waddling out of the feed room when they should have been locked up for the night in the hay barn. Ash said he'd unload the tack from the horsebox if I sorted out the ducks and gave Dolly some more hay. I pulled back the huge arched door, ready to shoo in the ducks, and decided to tell off Judy, the head groom, tomorrow for leaving them out.

I knew something was wrong before I even reached for the light. Sometimes you can instinctively feel a presence, another human being. The fluorescent light flashed erratically, flickered on and off and then lit up. Some bales had been moved out of place to form a temporary corral. There in the middle was a gorgeous piebald horse about 15.2 with the cutest face and the most enormous crested neck. He stared at me, dribbling a trail of hay, with his bottom lip hanging open making him look slightly gormless.

Curled up alongside him was a tall willowy girl wrapped in a sleeping bag, wearing a baseball cap. She stirred as the door clicked shut and then leapt up when she noticed the light.

"Stay back, keep back, I'm a karate black belt!" She was on her feet in seconds brandishing a plank of wood and trembling like a frightened deer. The piebald just stood and stared and then went back to eating.

"It's OK." I backed off, wondering whether she'd escaped from an asylum or whether she belonged to a group of travellers. "I'm not going to hurt you."

She was about five foot ten, very slim, and had slaty grey, almond-shaped eyes. Her hair was piled inside the hat. She reminded me of a giraffe that was being tracked by a lion.

Ash opened the door behind me, carrying a dressage saddle and bridle and looking as amazed as I was.

Recognition immediately filtered into the girl's eyes. "Oh, you're Ash Burgess." She dropped the plank and crumpled onto a bale of hay sobbing her heart out.

"Excuse me for asking," Ash stared at her, blank faced, "but who on earth are you?"

"You break the lock on our barn, you use it as some kind of dormitory, you smuggle in a horse who might have God knows what germs and now you tell me you're my new groom?"

Ash was pacing up and down the common

room, raking his hand through his hair and ignoring my gestures to control his temper.

There was something about this girl that told me she was in big trouble. She wasn't tough, she was just acting tough, and she genuinely seemed in a state.

"My name's Helen Taylor. I'm eighteen. Your head groom employed me."

She sat quivering from head to toe, twisting her hands nervously in her lap. "I'm supposed to start tomorrow."

"But we don't take horses." Ash looked out of the door to the spare stable where we'd put the piebald. "It's out of the question. You'll have to take him away."

The girl's face froze in alarm. Then she gathered up her rucksack and stood up. "Wherever I go, Beachball comes with me. I'll work every hour God sends, I'm experienced with horses, I don't need much money; but he's got to be part of the deal." She brushed away a tear and marched towards the door. "I'm sorry to have wasted your time."

"It's all right," I blurted out. "He can stay, it's no problem."

Ash shot me a glacial look but I'd backed him into a corner. "Oh all right, a month's trial, but make sure he has a flu jab and tetanus at your own cost. In the meantime keep him away from my eventers."

I winked at the girl and decided it was high time I introduced myself. "Alex Johnson," I said. "I'm Ash's girlfriend."

I don't know why I had to say that but it was almost as if I had to establish ground rules. In other words, "hands off". Helen smiled and held out her hand. She was the first girl I'd ever noticed not take an immediate shine to Ash. She didn't bat her eyelashes or toss her hair. She just wasn't in the slightest bit interested. I instinctively knew we were going to hit it off big time.

Ash wasn't so sure. "There's something not quite right about her," he said as soon as Helen had gone out to settle Beachball for the night.

"That's just because she doesn't fancy you," I said, sitting on the pool table and kicking off my boots. "You're so used to female adoration that you need therapy when girls don't throw themselves at your feet."

He pulled me off the table and held me by my shoulders. "If Helen Taylor proves a disaster I'll hold you totally responsible."

"Fine."

I went off to check Barney before we turned off all the lights. I didn't tell Ash that there was something creepily familiar about Helen.

That I'd seen that chiselled elfin face somewhere before. Or that her hands were snow white and uncalloused. Helen Taylor had never done a day's stable work in her life. But I kept it all to myself.

CHAPTER TWO

"She's utterly hopeless." Zoe, my best friend, followed me into Barney's stable hissing in my ear, brandishing a pitchfork. "She doesn't know a dandy brush from a hoofpick – she didn't even know what a tack room is."

Helen had turned up an hour before anybody else with a carrier bag containing an apron, rubber gloves and a bottle of bleach. She seemed to think that being a groom was a bit like a cleaning job. You just grabbed the Flash and got down to it.

All morning we'd been trying to disguise her incompetence by getting her to do jobs like scrubbing out mangers and sweeping the yard. She was so nice and determined to do well that I had to help her. Besides, I didn't want to lose face in front of Ash. Judy was so busy settling in a batch of new horses that she didn't notice how Helen had hung up the bridles upside down and laid a saddle flat on the floor.

"Give her a chance," I snapped. "She's a fast learner, and she loves animals." Nigel and Reggie had taken to her from the start and followed her round devotedly from stable to stable.

Neither of us could understand why Helen had a horse as beautiful as Beachball but knew nothing about horse care. Every five minutes she went across to give him a hug and a pat. He was so soft and adorable it was impossible not to fall in love with him. He had great big paddly feet and a roman nose and every time he saw a new horse he'd squeal in excitement.

Helen sneaked back to his stable and stroked his big black and white head still wearing her rubber gloves with wisps of straw stuck to her baseball cap.

"Face it, Alex." Zoe watched her with exasperation. "She's not going to last two minutes."

Zoe and I had a lesson with Eric organized for that afternoon over at the Sutton Vale Pony Club showground. Some of the other members were coming along, which meant the training session would be shambolic from the very beginning.

Jasper Carrington was the biggest two-timing flirt in the area and his outrageous pranks put Camilla to shame. Unfortunately for us, his long-suffering girlfriend, Toukie, was in America visiting relatives, so in the meantime he was making a beeline for Zoe. I was determined to stop it. Zoe was just getting over a broken heart after being taken in by an event rider called Jack

Landers. The last thing she needed was Jasper playing his games.

We had lunch in the common room piled round a portable TV watching a big showjumping event and trying to guess John Whitaker's age. If I didn't become a famous event rider and win Olympic gold I'd die of disappointment.

The lunchtime news came on and Helen had a coughing fit and insisted we turn it off because she wanted us to go through all the horses' names one more time. We never thought that she was behaving suspiciously. We never dreamed she might be hiding something that would make national news.

Barney warmed up on the showground with Eric watching and to anybody else he would have looked perfect. But we both knew his heart wasn't in it.

"It's you," Eric bawled. "You've stopped enjoying it, you've lost your enthusiasm and it's translating to Barney. You're trying too hard."

"How can anybody try too hard?" I bawled back. "You're wrong, Eric. That's a load of bunkum."

"I don't mind you having an opinion," he grinned, "as long as it's the same as mine. Now get using those legs and turn up the centre line like a professional."

11

Zoe wasn't faring much better. She had a beautiful grey mare called Lace who was as good as gold, but Zoe never put enough effort into her riding to get anywhere. She was lolling around in sitting trot doing silly egg shapes and watching desperately for Jasper's horsebox.

"Zoe Jackson, you make a melon look like an athlete. Now get moving."

We spent the next fifteen minutes doing trotting poles which are supposed to regulate the pace and get the horse concentrating. Eric always said that when you have problems with your jumping you've got to go back to basics and rebuild your confidence. Barney was furious that we had to do such boring exercises. Some ponies love jumping so much that the sight of coloured poles was enough to get them excited, and Barney was one of them.

We had one pole on the ground and trotted a circle in front of it several times until he was relaxed and obedient. Then we trotted over the pole and went back onto the circle. Once Barney was doing this calmly we laid out three poles and repeated the process. If Barney went too fast I had to stay calm and simply go back to working on a circle. It took endless patience.

Zoe was tearing her hair out trying to get Lace to rein back. Moving backwards is always difficult for a horse and overdoing it can get them into the nasty habit of running backwards whenever they feel like it. Eric ordered one of the other riders to place two poles in the centre of the schooling area so that Zoe could rein back between them.

"Now remember," Eric yelled as Zoe strained her eyes towards an approaching Range Rover and trailer, "stay straight, don't rush, ask only for a few steps and then move forward straight away."

Camilla Davis, our other friend who kept her pony, The Hawk, at the stables, leapt out of the back of the Range Rover shrieking instructions to her mother. Eric's jaw dropped open in alarm. She was wearing a swimming costume, jodhpurs and a bum bag containing a mobile phone.

"Lord give me strength." Eric buried his head in his hands as Cam howled with disappointment that we weren't going beach riding. "This is a training session, not a knees-up," Eric growled. "Next thing you'll be wearing trainers, floppy earrings and a kiss-me-quick hat and telling me you look perfectly OK to go across country."

Cam pulled a face and answered her phone. It was her latest boyfriend, Simon.

Just when Eric was about to despair, Jasper Carrington pounded through the main gates on his hyperactive liver chestnut who in my opinion needed to be on tranquillizers and Jasper on something similar. Zoe blushed and gave up on reining back.

Jasper pulled up, reins in one hand, with his eyes latched on to Zoe who was now visibly trembling. Jasper was blond, tall, muscular and extremely rich and by everybody's account, a real womanizer. It was almost as if he had to pull girls to prove his attraction, and his lovable roguish personality won them over every time. But Zoe was falling hard.

Jasper gave her a terrific smile and rode over, gently caressing her neck when Eric wasn't watching. Three other girls on fat ponies looked as if they were drooling into their boots.

Mrs Davis, Cam's mother, was waiting in the Range Rover, devouring the centre spread of the *Daily Mail*. Nobody knew the significance of what she was reading. I had no idea that my life was on the verge of being turned upside down. Mrs Davis read on, totally absorbed, soaking up every detail.

We went out onto the cross-country course and did some pretty decent jumping over log combinations but as soon as Eric asked me to jump a three-foot-three spread I went to pieces. Every time we jumped it we took off at a different place. Barney was getting more and more agitated and at the third attempt he dug in his heels at the last minute.

The half dozen riders standing watching from

the Sutton Vale Pony Club were smirking their heads off and if it wasn't for bucket loads of spirit and obstinacy I'd have burst out crying there and then.

Surprisingly Eric didn't lose his temper but pulled out his notepad and started scribbling frantically on a sheet of paper.

"Here we go again." Jasper pulled a face and a girl with plaits asked him if his hair was naturally so blond. "If you're trying to chat me up, forget it," he sneered lazily, chewing at his nails. "My heart belongs to Toukie and I'm going to stay faithful."

Zoe looked instantly mortified. Jasper winked at her and I noticed he'd got his fingers crossed behind his back.

"Here." Eric passed me the paper. "Read this. You're forgetting that the main objective is to get over the jump. You're thinking so much about balance and keeping him straight and riding out of the corner, that you're forgetting to kick on. The priority is always to go forward. Now try again."

I did exactly as Eric said and this time Barney went soaring over without a second thought. After that we disbanded and went back to the horseboxes. Cam's mother had been sunbathing in a fold-up chair and instantly started fussing over The Hawk who was dancing sideways and working himself into a right lather over a bay mare he seemed to fancy. "Have you forgotten how much that pony cost?" she nagged.

While she was bragging in a loud voice about The Hawk's value, Daisy, Eric's dog, wandered over and chewed up her Daily Mail and her wing-shaped sunglasses.

Cam loaded up The Hawk in an obvious temper and, just to annoy her mother, she stripped off her jodhpurs and waddled around in her skimpy cossie so Jasper's eyes nearly popped out of his head.

Zoe and I rode home both trying to devour choc ices while holding on to the reins. It was hot and sticky. We turned down a bridle path to stay out of the traffic and walked the last mile home so Barney and Lace could cool off.

Zoe sulked because I wouldn't agree that Jasper was a good catch and because I burst out laughing when she suggested having a perm.

"Oh that's so typical of you," she snarled. "You're so beautiful: the perfect hair which just falls into place, no spots, the perfect body. Well, everybody's not as lucky as you, Alex. We're not all golden people."

My jaw dropped open in shock. Zoe was usually so easy going. I really thought we were back to being friends after the bad feeling over Jack Landers.

"Just leave it," Zoe pouted, pushing Lace into canter. "You're so used to being the best you can't imagine anything else."

We rode into the yard in silence, put the horses in the stables and carried the tack into the common room.

Judy was over by the sink wrestling with a double bridle which looked as if it had fallen into a bucket of water.

"That girl is absolutely hopeless," she hissed. "Look at this bridle, it's ruined." It was a two-toned leather bridle, which was made more for appearance than anything else. "How can a girl have references like hers and be so hopeless? Well, I'm not going to lose my job over Helen Taylor." She took a swig of cold scummy coffee. "She's just going to have to buck up her ideas."

"Where is she now?" I asked, trying not to sound too concerned.

"She went out on Beachball. Or at least she tried to go out. You ought to have seen her reins – like washing lines."

I scrubbed up my grooming kit and gave Barney an hour's grooming. Zoe went home and Judy left shortly after. There was just the odd livery owner floating around. Jenny was trying to lunge Gypsy Fair, her scatty thoroughbred who was always having mystery illnesses. There was still no sign of Helen. She could have done a runner. I checked inside the barn and her sleeping bag and a baggy jumper were still there in a corner. She must be coming back.

I helped Jenny for a while, then decided to raid Ash's Jeep for some chocolate and a can of Coke. He always had a supply stocked under the seat. There resting on the dashboard was an unopened *Daily Express* and *Horse and Hound*. I took both and three bars of chocolate and made for the garden where I collapsed under a cool willow tree. *Horse and Hound* was full of the Olympics with endless articles analysing our failure to win a team Gold in the eventing after such a good lead. I gleaned every bit of information I could and then turned to the *Daily Express* with the sole intention of reading the telly page and my daily horoscope.

The page fell open as if by fate. I blinked twice and then read on, totally hooked, unable to believe my eyes. It couldn't be; it was incredible. This kind of thing didn't happen on your doorstep. But I studied the photograph and I was convinced.

I felt so disorientated. No wonder I felt as if I'd seen her before. Right on cue Beachball plodded into the yard, his head lolling half asleep in the heat. Helen looked like any normal person coming back off a hack. I'd have to confront her, there was no other way.

I waited until she'd gone into the stable and

then followed her in. She turned round, surprised, tugging at the girth buckles without success. "Hi. I thought you'd have gone home . . ." She saw the newspaper in my hand.

"How on earth did you think you'd get away with it?" I stared at her with cold eyes wanting an honest answer.

"I didn't, I just wanted to buy a bit of time. I didn't expect the papers to get hold of it so fast."

Her face was crumpling in panic now, her long gazelle legs quivering with the shock of being discovered. She still didn't really resemble the glamorous girl in the picture, with backcombed hair and heavy make-up, wearing a designer suit.

"It's you, isn't it?" I stared at the new groom with dawning horror. "You're the supermodel who's gone missing. You're Jade Lamond."

She pulled off her baseball cap letting ice-blonde hair spill out to her waist. "If you tell anyone, you'll put Beachball's life in danger. Swear to me, Alex, swear you'll keep quiet."

"Just tell me one thing. Why, why here and a groom of all things?"

She flickered her lovely grey eyes and for the first time I noticed her lashes had been dyed. "I've been in front of the cameras since I was fourteen. I've been all over the world. I've been bullied and controlled and dictated to. I just want to be free.

Does that answer your question? I want to be normal, Alex. Like you. You must help me."

"I think you've got some explaining to do." I squinted my eyes trying to take everything in. "First of all, I must know – how can Beachball possibly be in danger?"

CHAPTER THREE

I took her to see Eric. It was the only thing I could think of. Eric would know what to do. He always had an answer for everything.

Helen or rather Jade was on the verge of tears and practically hysterical that she'd been found out: "You don't understand, I can't go back."

Eric's cottage was isolated, tucked away behind the wood on the Burgess estate. Nobody would see us. It was the perfect retreat. Eric had to put on his glasses before he could read the headline blaring out of the paper: "Supermodel Jade Lamond Goes Missing".

Jade crouched on the settee playing nervously with her incredible hair, her eyes bloodshot and panic stricken.

"I can't go back to him." Jade started pacing up and down. "He's a slavedriver, he treats me like a machine."

"But surely you realized it would only be a matter of time before you were discovered." Eric stroked Daisy's floppy ears trying to take in the saga.

"No, no, I didn't. I look so different without

make-up. And I didn't think Monty would go to the press. I didn't think he'd be that stupid." She sat down again on the settee, bending her legs slightly to one side, her back ramrod stiff. It was obvious she was a model: her posture was perfect. I was surprised that I hadn't noticed it before.

"I bought Beachball a few weeks ago when I was up in Blackpool appearing at the British Golf Open. He was being used for rides in these stupid buggies. He looked exhausted. I had to rescue him. Anyway, I took him to London and put him in a stables at Hyde Park. It cost a fortune but I was so in love with him. I was even buying him special treats from Harrods. It was the first time I had someone to love. Do you know, I've never had a boyfriend. Monty would never allow it. He didn't want me to lose my innocent vulnerable look. Can you believe it, I'm eighteen and I feel like a child. I've never even been kissed."

"So Monty is your manager?" I had to get all the facts straight.

"Yes." Jade rubbed her hands over her eyes and curled up her legs. "He's my jailor. I was supposed to fly out to New York for a big promotion but I disappeared for a couple of days. I didn't want to leave Beachball. When Monty found me he said if I didn't go to New York and let him sort out Beachball he'd shoot him and be done with it. When I refused he went out for a couple of hours and came back with a twelve bore rifle. He's deadly serious. He's going to kill Beachball."

She broke down in tears and I went to make some tea and poured loads of sugar in it. "Here, this'll make you feel better."

Daisy was slobbering all over Jade's jeans and looking up at her adoringly. "This is so cosy," she said. "I've never known such a beautiful cottage. It's so homely."

Scraps of Jade's past were floating back to me now from an article I'd read in a teenage mag. "You're an orphan, aren't you?" I blurted out. "Your parents were killed in a car crash."

"Yes, that's right, I'm a St Barnabas baby. I was shopping in the local supermarket when I was fourteen and someone from Monty's agency approached me. They said I could make a lot of money. I was in the middle of trying to find the smallest block of cheddar cheese. It seemed like a godsend."

I gulped down syrupy tea myself and tried to come to terms with having a supermodel in Eric's front room. I was dying to ask what Naomi Campbell was really like and whether she knew Kate Moss but I didn't dare.

Eric read my thoughts and scowled deeply. "There's nothing to be gained from running away," he said. "Miss Lamond, I really do think you're going to have to tell this Monty character where you are before somebody else does. It doesn't mean you have to go back to him. We'll protect you. We'll help you all we can. I despise bullies and this Monty sounds like one of the worst."

"Oh you're so lovely, both of you." She reached across and squeezed my hand. "But I can't. I know you mean well but I'm contracted for another three years. Monty is calling all the shots. He'll make me go back in front of the cameras."

"Now listen to me, young lady. Nobody, and I mean nobody, has to do something they don't want to do. I may be in a wheelchair but bullies like Monty do not scare me. Is that clear?"

She grinned for the first time all night. Without the baseball cap she really did have the most beautiful face. "Oh, Alex." She squeezed my hand again and welled up with tears. "I'd give anything to swap places with you."

It was only much later that I realized the true significance of that statement.

"What's going on?" Zoe came running down the stable yard the next morning. There were press cars and television people all over. Ash was trying to fend off a pushy dark-haired girl with a mike and George, one of the event horses, was leaning over the fence chewing away on someone's very expensive looking equipment and loving all the excitement.

Jade was right at my side, trembling like a puppy, and constantly saying "no comment". She rammed down her baseball cap and grabbed my arm. "Ignore them." She gritted her teeth. "Don't let them draw you, don't look in their cameras."

Jade had stayed the night in our spare bedroom and my dad had dropped us off at the end of the drive. He hadn't seen the group of lurking paparazzi and neither had we. They pounced as soon as we were by ourselves.

"Someone's spilled the beans." Jade carried on marching, dragging me along with her, showing spirit I didn't know she had. "This is my life," she shrugged, yet again reading my thoughts. "Isn't it the pits?"

"Are you one of Jade's modelling friends?" A reporter with a pony tail pushed forward, practically sticking his face in mine. "Have you been harbouring Jade? How long have you known her? Do you work for Monty?"

Someone else loomed up on my right. "Leave me alone!" I lifted my arm to cover my face and then saw Ash bounding through the sea of bodies, his face anxious and drawn.

"Get out of their way. You heard her, leave them alone." He slapped a hand over someone's camera. "This is private property, now back off."

They seemed to get the message. Ash grabbed hold of my hand, a tower of strength, and my

25

panic immediately simmered down. Jade laughed that I had my own private bodyguard and asked if she could hire him some day. That was Ash; he could irritate me to death and wind me up to distraction but when push came to shove he was always there – he'd never let me down yet.

I could see Jade was just putting on a face, that she must be going through turmoil inside. These reporters just never gave up, they were like a flock of vultures, swooping round ready to prey on anything.

"There's somebody to see you." Ash squeezed my hand while scanning Jade's face, obviously curious now he knew who she was. "You should have told me," he said. "We should have been prepared for all this. You've taken on a job under false pretences."

"Oh Ash, don't be so pompous." I felt like kicking him. "All this publicity will have new owners flocking in, not to mention boosting your name."

I jogged along next to both of them, feeling like a midget. In heels Jade would be taller than Ash. Barney stuck his head over his door and neighed as soon as he saw us. Beachball did the same.

Jade was just about to go across to them when a man in a pinstriped suit leapt out of a BMW parked near the office.

"Hello, Jade. Long time no see."

He was blond with a broad face and coldish eyes and a distinctive presence. He smelled of money. "Aren't you going to introduce me to your little friends?"

I despised him from that moment on. He treated her like a child.

"Ash, Alex, I'd like to introduce you to my manager, Monty Brentford."

It was obvious the effect he was having on Jade. She was ghostly pale and was frantically chewing on her nails, unable to meet his eyes.

"How many times have I told you not to do that?" He tapped her hand away from her mouth and Jade backed up a couple of steps, trembling.

I thought it was my imagination when he kept glancing at me with X-ray eyes roving up and down my body. Camilla and Zoe were spying from the common room window. Two of the livery owners were sweeping up round the stables just so they could get closer.

"So how did you find me?" Jade threw the question at him.

"The local rag rang me this morning – somebody here at the stables tipped them off. Obviously you don't have as many friends as you think."

"Look, if you don't mind we've all got work to do." Ash shifted his weight from one foot to the other. "Can you please just buzz off!"

"Five minutes." Monty clasped Jade's arm. "We'll go for a walk, dear. You seem to enjoy going walkabout."

"It's OK. I'll be all right." Jade flashed me a backwards glance. "Keep an eye on Beachball."

"It was you, wasn't it?" I rounded on Ash as soon as they were out of earshot. "You phoned the papers, you knew all the time."

I couldn't believe he'd stoop so low.

"Oh all right, yes it was. I checked her references when I started to get suspicious and then I read the *Mail* at the dentist's."

"She's a really nice girl." I was fuming. My blood pressure was soaring. "How could you, Ash? You're just capitalizing on her bad fortune. Honestly, you make me sick."

"Bad fortune indeed – she must be loaded." Ash watched Jade disappear down the drive. "She's no lame duck, Alex. She's a prima donna looking for attention. If you ask me all this is probably a set-up to get publicity. Famous people organize stunts like this all the time. It's just par for the course."

"If you didn't run these stables I'd disown you," I yelled.

"And you're too gullible, Alex, believe me. I know what I'm talking about."

"I don't believe you." I stomped off towards

Barney who looked as if he was passing out with hunger.

Jenny came in to borrow my hoof pick and commented on how beautiful Jade was. "It's all a bit of a commotion, isn't it? I wonder how much she's getting paid for all this."

Jenny was a widow in her fifties and scatty beyond belief. Even she thought the worst. "Jenny," I said, pulling back Barney's rugs while he devoured his breakfast. "What does 'gullible' mean?"

"I could make you into an overnight star. You've got what it takes, kid – you could be the new look for the nineties."

It wasn't a dream. Monty Brentford was sitting opposite me in Ash's office offering the chance of a lifetime. To become a top model.

"Just a few hours over the summer holidays, nothing too overpowering. We can do a shoot with your nag if it makes you feel any happier."

This would be a way of raising money for a dressage saddle, a new bridle – hey, who knows, maybe my own horsebox. Alex Johnson. Paris. London. New York.

"You've got cheekbones to die for." Jade narrowed her eyes as she scrutinized my face. "Good thick hair, although it needs a decent cut, but that's no problem. Fantastic skin, a nice smile. It could work."

"But . . . but, Jade . . ."

"Listen, about earlier, I was probably over-reacting. I'm stressed out from too much work. I exaggerated. I'd be nothing without Monty." She ran a hand through her luscious hair, pressing together fuchsia lips. But her eyes wouldn't meet mine. "I'm going to have a few weeks off, enjoying some time with Beachball. This would be a fantastic opportunity, Alex, once in a lifetime."

She was right. I'd be a fool to turn it down. Monty leaned over the table, seeing me weaken. "If you'd like, we could organize a horse wagon, get your pony to the beach and do a shoot. If you don't like it you can tell the photographer to take a running jump and still enjoy a day at the seaside. What do you think?"

"Well, it sounds fantastic, but I'll have to ask my parents, and then there's my boyfriend."

"You're not married to him, are you? What's it got to do with him?"

"Well . . ."

"Just say the word and I'll be straight on to the photographer. We can whisk you off to the hairdresser's this afternoon. Jade, find the nearest horse shop – we'll need a whole load of gear."

"So you'll really have Barney in the pictures?"

"Scout's honour." Monty saluted me and then

winked. I noticed his eyes were each a different colour.

"The horse will give it a novel angle. There aren't too many models who look great on a horse. You're going to be a natural. Trust me."

If I'd been a bit older and a bit wiser I'd have realized those two words spelt trouble. But Jade seemed to think it was OK. I trusted her even if I didn't trust Monty. And what had I got to lose? Here was a chance for Barney and me to become famous. And rich!

My mind was made up. I stuck out my right hand and shook on the deal. I was on the yellow brick road to all my dreams.

"Welcome to the world of modelling." Monty lit a cigar, striking the match off his shoe. "This time next year, Alex Johnson could be the next Kate Moss!"

CHAPTER FOUR

"Are you crazy?" Ash was grooming Donavon when I broke the news. "Have you completely lost it?" Even with a deep suntan he seemed to go pale.

"It's no big deal." I shrugged my shoulders trying to be cool but ending up just feeling guilty.

"Tell me this is a wind-up?" He stared straight into my eyes and I could see the disappointment when he realized I was deadly serious.

"And what about Barney? Yesterday he was the centre of your universe. Where does he fit in to your jet-set plans?"

"It's all right, I'll have plenty of time to do both. I'm doing this for him, so I'll have more money."

Ash narrowed his eyes. "I really thought I knew you, Alex. I thought you were horse mad and dedicated to a career in horses. Now you spring it on me that you want to be a model. And you know something?" I cringed when I saw the pain and hurt in his eyes. "I don't think I know you at all."

I raced round rearranging Barney's bedding and filling his hay net to bursting so it would last the rest of the day. Barney made me feel worse by standing with his back to me and refusing to have his ears rubbed which usually proved irresistible. I promised I'd ride him as soon as I got back from the hairdresser's but he just scowled at me and showed more interest in licking out his manger.

The taxi pulled into the yard with Jade in the back wearing supercool sunglasses and her hair all piled up. Her eyes were red as if she'd been crying, but I was too busy thinking about the best tack shop in town and how Monty had promised that I could keep whatever horsey clothes he bought for the photo shoot.

The smell of leather was overpowering as we stepped through the door. For years I'd been coming into this tack shop and mooning over all the beautiful jackets and bridles and leather head collars.

The manageress with a tight perm and even tighter lips puckered them up into a sour scowl as the door clicked shut and she recognized me. I'd usually loiter around for an hour or so examining all the latest gadgets from plastic mangers to electric grooming machines and then buy a bar of saddle soap or some fly spray.

This time I marched straight over to the rack of jodhpurs and expertly flicked through, trying to disguise the fact that my hands were shaking.

Monty immediately brought out a wad of credit cards and the manageress coughed excitedly and scuttled out from behind the counter.

"And what would Sir be most interested in?" she gushed, making me want to be sick. Jade rolled her eyes at me and I stifled a giggle.

"I want your most expensive jodhpurs, leather boots, black riding jacket and some fancy shirts. Those over there will do." The price tags I knew by heart and started at £120.

Monty had explained when he jumped in the taxi that he wanted to put together an overnight portfolio and send it off to the designer names in horse wear. "If we can get you some top jobs with a couple of big designers we can branch out from there. How would you fancy modelling with Guy Goosen? I'm trying to put together a deal at the moment."

I felt tiny electric shocks shoot through my body and then Jade was holding up a fantastic black bomber jacket with a horse's head on the back in gold. "I think this is perfect."

I ended up with three different pairs of jodhpurs, one in a kind of powder blue suede, another just plain white skintight and another a very light rusty beige corduroy. They showed off the length of my legs but seemed to disguise my bony knees. I had two polo shirts, a white show shirt and a black jacket that fitted to perfection. The one I had at home was two inches short in the sleeves and was so tight around the chest that it made me feel hunchbacked.

The manageress was goggle-eyed and flapping around with carrier bags unable to find a large enough size. Monty let me buy a head collar in best English leather with brass buckles and a green lead rope. Barney was going to look the cat's whiskers.

I felt as if I was floating on air as Monty pulled out his American Express card and asked the manageress to throw in a pair of chaps. I felt like the luckiest girl in the world – as if I'd won the lottery.

Half an hour later they were dropping me off outside the hairdresser's and I stood teetering on the pavement, patting my long locks wondering how much "Pierre" had been told to chop off. Just before I got cold feet the door pushed open and a girl with stark black hair clutching a pack of rollers asked if I was lost.

Pierre was dark, moody and gorgeous and his fingers running through my hair made me feel like Cindy Crawford. Everybody was talking about the Lamond girl who had been discovered hiding out at a riding stables. I slithered down in my chair and pretended to be absorbed in an article in *In the Saddle*.

Then, just as Pierre was applying the finishing

touches, Ash's jeep pulled up outside on double yellow lines and he burst through the door with Daisy on her lead so she wouldn't sit in the back chewing up the seats.

"What do you think you're doing?" he bellowed, looking absolutely furious and not caring who was listening. His shirt and jodhpurs were soaking wet all down the front and there was a green weed hanging out of his boot. "You didn't shut Barney's door properly. He's been charging round the village and we found him in Mrs Carrington's duck pond. She's threatening to sue us for negligence. And what on earth have you done to your hair? You look ridiculous."

"It's an Anthea Turner look," I thundered as we piled into the jeep and set off, nearly crashing into an open-topped bus. "I like it and that's all that matters."

"I'd have thought you'd have been more interested in your horse," he growled. "Knowing Barney he's probably wolfed all of the Carringtons' goldfish."

Horror flooded over me in a series of sickly waves as I stared at Barney over his stable door. He wasn't a yellow dun any more, he was a slimy green. And his mane and tail were bedraggled, with a water lily trailing along the ground. Even worse, he ponged to high heaven; he could have put a skunk to shame.

"Oh Barney, what have you done to me?"

The photo shoot was at 9.30 the next morning. It was now five o'clock in the evening. "We'll have to bath him," I wailed, picking bits of greenery out of his ears.

"We?" Ash flicked back his hair in despair. "How did I get roped into this? I'm the innocent party."

"You're my boyfriend." I slipped on Barney's head collar. "It's what boyfriends do."

I told him I had some horse shampoo and conditioner in my grooming box.

"Never mind that." Ash bristled with sarcasm. "You'd better fetch the bleach and disinfectant."

Bathing a horse was never easy and Ash ended up switching on the hosepipe for the final rinse. The worst of the green stains were round his fetlocks and on the side of his neck.

"What kind of horse jumps in a duck pond and pretends he's the Loch Ness Monster?" Ash irritably flipped a wet sponge in my direction.

By now my fantastic hairdo was in ruins.

"Just keep scrubbing," I grunted, wanting to sit down and cry.

"Well, you know what they say." Ash deliberately ruffled my hair with a soapy hand. "Pets always resemble their owners, which suggests that you, my darling, are wild, uncontrollable, and per-

37

manently leaping into trouble with both feet. Am I right?"

I quickly poured horse shampoo all over his head to prove a point. "Of course, dear. Aren't you always?"

It didn't take long to towel dry Barney's face and mane and swish round his tail. I put the hairdryer on his heels just to be safe because they easily became cracked and dry if I just left them damp.

By the end of all this Barney looked like a new pin which helped lessen my feeling of guilt that because I hadn't exercised him all day it was hardly surprising he'd decided to do it himself. Ash had to answer the phone twice to nosy reporters hoping to catch Jade on the line. I was wilting fast with hunger and exhaustion and then I suddenly remembered it was Jasper Carrington's tack-swapping party and Zoe had made me promise to turn up with at least two items of equipment. The idea was for everybody to take something they didn't want, like a numnah, a snaffle, jodhpurs that were too small, and swap it for something else. Zoe had been carrying on as if nobody had ever had the idea before and it was the most important social event in the Sutton Vale Pony Club diary. I'd have to go. All I really wanted to do was go home, steam my face and have an early night.

The thought of facing Mrs Carrington and explaining how Barney hadn't meant to wreck her pond was making me edgy and irritable. Especially as I'd been home to my parents with Ash and my dad was rattling out questions all about Jade and whether I knew what I was doing. My mother, who always spoilt Barney rotten and even made his favourite flapjack, thought it was brilliant to have some professional photographs. "Anyway," she poked my dad on the shoulder, "she's got Ash to look after her."

The Carringtons lived in a big, modern, white house on the edge of Ash's village. We were three hours late and all we had between us was a pelham, a saddle cloth which didn't fit Barney's saddle and a horsey sweatshirt which had a tiny hoof oil stain on the sleeve.

We parked the jeep and went inside, Ash striding ahead and insisting that we weren't going to stay long. The party seemed to have gravitated towards the indoor swimming pool although there was a couple snogging on the bottom stair and a girl called Spanner in the kitchen who was putting make-up on Damien Bevan and taking a long time applying the lipstick. Mr and Mrs Carrington must have been out.

Jasper sauntered through from the swimming pool in a pair of skimpy trunks. "Oh Alex, good of you to visit us. The fish are outside, needing mouth-to-mouth resuscitation. Dad's old carp looks as if it's had a stroke."

I went red and thrust the sweatshirt, bit and saddle cloth into his arms. Jasper's eyes always had that too intimate look in them and I always ended up looking down at my feet. He slapped Ash on the back and then asked me what I was in training for, horseback snorkling or underwater polo?

I steered Ash towards the food and while we were raiding the pizza slices we suddenly got invaded by half the pony club asking about Jade.

"Is it really true?" asked a mousy girl.

Jasper said he couldn't wait to meet her and maybe I could give her his phone number. The girl gazed into his eyes like a puppy. Zoe was over by the trestle tables rooting through tack and looking terribly efficient.

I started wandering across but got waylaid by a ginger-haired guy I hadn't met before inviting everybody to his 16th birthday party in a marquee.

Jasper howled with laughter behind me and asked him how he was going to fill it and whether the guests were going to talk to each other with walkie-talkies and pass the jelly round on a motor-bike. The poor guy quailed and I kicked Jasper hard just above the ankle.

"Alex, so good of you to turn up – three hours late." Zoe appeared at my side, obviously having witnessed the whole thing. "I know you don't like Jasper," she hissed, "but couldn't you just try for once, for me."

The next hour limped past with Ash managing to do a swap and ending up with a pair of black rubber reins. I got caught with a geek wearing shorts and a bum bag who either had a sore throat or was trying to talk in a husky voice and convince me he had the makings of a male model.

Jasper and Zoe were clinging to each other like vines. Somebody had spilt the beans about my photo shoot at the beach and the atmosphere had turned positively icy.

"Jealousy runs amok," Ash whispered in my ear. "I hope it's worth losing all your friends over."

I couldn't believe that everybody had turned so cold.

"Come on, drink up and let's get out of here." Ash clinked my glass with his own.

"But I can't just leave Zoe thinking I don't care," I said.

I looked round hastily for my best friend who seemed to have done a disappearing act. Jasper was over by a yucca plant chatting to Spanner who was twiddling her top button seductively. "He's at it again," I fumed. "As soon as Zoe turns her back."

Jasper leaned against the yucca, momentarily lost his balance and recovered. "Did you know

41

that a lion can make love up to seventy times in one day?"

"Right, that does it." My blood was boiling. "I'm going to sort out that slippery lech if it's the last thing I do." I passed my drink to Ash and marched over to Jasper.

"Oh, if it isn't the budding model who keeps bad-mouthing me to the whole of the female population. You know, Alex, I think you've secretly got the hots for me."

It didn't go unnoticed that he'd recently got changed into a white Armani shirt and jeans which he'd been boasting about for the last half hour.

"I'm warning you, Jasper, if you hurt Zoe . . ."

He shot me a charming grin but with an edge as sharp as steel. "What are you, her personal bodyguard or something?"

Without thinking I stuck out my hand, pushed him in the chest and sent him sprawling into the pool.

Everybody turned round, amazed. Spanner was on her knees extending a fleshy hand to Jasper who was spluttering and splashing around like a hooked fish.

"How could you?" Zoe was directly behind me. She was carrying a jug of orange juice awash with ice cubes which were clinking as her hand shook.

"Just what is your problem, Alex? Are you determined to ruin my love life?"

Ash stepped in and tried to explain, but Zoe interrupted. "Oh, don't you stick up for her. She's got you wrapped round her little finger."

"But Zoe . . ."

"Don't but me. I'm in love with Jasper, and he loves me. We're an item and you're just going to have to accept it."

Jasper heaved himself out of the pool, dripping wet but gloating that Zoe and I were having a stand-up row in front of the whole of the Pony Club.

"Would you please leave now." Zoe bit down on her lip, her nose twitching as it did when she was angry. She wouldn't look at me. Neither would anybody else.

Ash grabbed my hand and dragged me away. "You've really blown it now." He held open the door of the jeep for me. "What on earth made you do that? It was like shooting yourself in the foot."

I crumpled with exhaustion and every last dreg of spirit drained out of me. Ash looked as if he wanted to strangle me with the rubber reins.

"Come here you, little monster." He grabbed hold of my shirt top and pulled me close, his eyes softening and dancing bemusedly. "You're untameable, do you know that? You're like a wild two year-old."

"Oh, Ash." I buried my head into his warm neck breathing in his aftershave in reassuring waves. "Apart from Jade you're the only friend I've got left."

He put both hands on my shoulders and looked straight into my eyes, his own suddenly flecked with concern. "But are you absolutely sure that Jade is your friend?"

CHAPTER FIVE

"Big smile, turn his head around, hold still, that's a sweetie."

The sea lapped gently at the sand a few yards away as the photographer dropped to his knees in front of us, and dramatically angled the camera for a new shot.

I'd never been so surrounded by people and so much the centre of attention. A make-up artist kept dabbing at my chin and cheeks and rearranging my hair after every five minutes. Monty was watching over everything, and giving everybody a rollicking for the slightest error. Apart from myself, that is. He was being as nice as pie.

Jade was a pillar of strength, giving me invaluable tips on how to pose. Ash had brought Donavon along for some exercise and to keep Barney company and there was a distinctly frosty atmosphere between him and Monty when I wasn't allowed to wear a riding hat and Ash thought it was ridiculous and dangerous. The only thing that lightened everybody up was when some seaside donkeys plodded along and Barney froze in terror and nearly leapt into the photographer's arms.

Then he took off up the beach and I could barely stop because he was in a different bridle with a rubber bit. He promptly dumped me near a windbreaker which I thought he was going to jump, and my hair trailed in the wet sand.

Monty was not amused. It took a good hour to get a sweating Barney and myself looking half decent and by that time the wind had got up and it had started to rain. I had enough hair spray applied to withstand a force ten gale.

Ash went off along the pier having put Donavon back in the horsebox and returned with fish and chips all round extra salted and with gallons of vinegar. The photographer who'd briefly mentioned earlier that he was a vegetarian polished off more cod than anybody.

Barney was in a mood for causing trouble. It was almost as if he thought modelling was poncey and unmanly. I wondered if Donavon had been winding him up. We wanted to take a shot in the sea which was all very well but Barney refused to come out and kept splashing water up all over the photographer and his camera.

"Come on, Kit, that's it. Let's call it a day, the nag's had enough."

Monty jumped into his car looking sour faced and giving me no indication as to whether the pictures were OK.

"Manners maketh man," Ash grimaced and

helped me untack Barney. I would never have dreamed how hard modelling could be. It was so tedious getting the right shots, especially with a horse who wouldn't stand still. Barney looked delighted with himself.

Jade came across grinning, her hair pulled back in a pony tail and her eyes shining. "You did brilliantly." She patted Barney when he stuffed his nose in her face for attention. "And so did you. Those pictures are going to be red hot. You'll have no end of jobs, Alex. I'm almost jealous."

"You!" I stared down at her, wondering if she was being patronizing. She was after all mega-famous.

"Yes, me. I remember a time when I lived for the camera, I loved it. Now I'm Jade by name and jaded by nature. Did you know my original name really was Helen Taylor? I'm thinking of going back to it."

We trundled back to the stables behind a seemingly endless convoy of tractors and com-bines, Ash crashing the gears and tooting wildly.

Monty had gone back to the hotel where he was staying and Ash was driving the horsebox with Jade crammed in between us.

It was only an hour back to the yard and Ash was contemplating taking the horses regularly to the beach for gallops. "If it was good enough for

Red Rum it's good enough for Donavon and Barney."

In fact I couldn't understand why we hadn't done it before. Sea water is brilliant for hardening and soothing horses' legs and can often work miracles with any lameness.

Judy was in the yard over by the manege as Ash manoeuvred the huge cream Lambourn horsebox into its position by the barn.

We hadn't even got the ramp down before she came tearing across, Nigel and Reggie following at her heels, quacking as they picked up on her panic.

"I don't know how to explain this," she said, dithering and not meeting anybody's eyes. I'd never seen her so tense.

"Dolly?" Ash's voice faded weakly into the air. The beautiful fleabitten ex-polo pony was the apple of his eye. He looked as if someone had just punched him in the stomach.

"No, no, not Dolly." Judy lifted her milky green eyes and looked straight at Jade. "It's Beach-ball. I was out on a hack with George and when I came back he'd gone. He's vanished!"

Jade went as stiff as a corpse.

"I'm so sorry." Judy was on the verge of tears. "This has never happened to me before. I've been out all day looking for him. I've been everywhere, I've rung the police. Nobody's seen a thing."

She was winding herself up into hysteria. Ash

48

put his arms round her and she burst into tears, loud racking sobs, mascara and eye shadow immediately smudging onto Ash's shirt. "How can a horse just disappear?"

"He hasn't." Jade tossed back her head so her silver mane of hair glinted exotically in the light. "He hasn't just disappeared – he's been taken, and I know who by. I'll bet my bottom dollar on it." Her words came out like icicles. Temper was building up inside her. "He's doing it again, he's controlling my life. He thinks he can do anything he likes."

"Jade, I think you'd better explain." Thoughts were racing through my mind.

"I don't have to. This is the moron who can give you all the answers."

Monty Brentford drove into the yard to pick Jade up. He braked hard scraping the gravel which I knew always annoyed Ash.

"All right, where is he?" Jade was burning up. She wrenched open the car door and I thought she was going to bodily drag Monty out. "It's not going to work, Monty. I'm quitting and nothing you do is going to stop me. If you've hurt a hair on his head I swear to God I'll turn that rifle on you."

"Hey hey, steady. You'll get a reputation for being neurotic." He was looking down his nose at Jade and she knew it.

"What have you done with him?" she glared ferociously. "I'm warning you, Brentford. You'd better tell me where he is. He's my baby."

"That you paid for with my money if I remember." Monty smiled apologetically to Ash and reached for an envelope inside the car. "If you must know, I've sent him back to Hyde Park. I thought that's what you wanted."

"Oh really? Don't I have a mind of my own then?" For a second I thought Jade was going to hit him. "It's funny how you waited till nobody was around. Very suspicious."

"Merely coincidence. I had no idea you wanted to carry on being a groom. Now if you don't mind, I've got something to discuss with Miss Johnson." Monty turned his back on her with such rudeness I was flabbergasted. How could he hijack Beachball like that?

Ash's face showed he was thinking exactly the same thing. He strode after Jade who was heading off towards the common room.

"Now before you get uppity..." Monty narrowed his eyes at me obviously sensing my outrage, "I've got an assignment for you. Do you know Blake Kildaire?"

My ears immediately flapped like an African elephant's. Blake Kildaire was one of the best young showjumpers in the country and utterly, divinely, unbelievably gorgeous.

"Well he's finally agreed to do a photo shoot for *In the Saddle*." Monty knew he'd got me hooked, all he had to do now was reel me in. "The thing is, they're looking for a young female model who can ride to pose with him. It's for the front cover. Horse Flair Wear are providing all the clothes. I said you might be interested."

"Might be!" My eyes were sticking out on stalks. "I'd give my right arm for a job like that. Are you sure they'd really be interested in me?"

"All you have to do is say yes." Monty's eyes gleamed with excitement, mirroring my own.

There was no way I could turn down an offer like that. Blake Kildaire was on a par with Keanu Reeves. I ignored all my instincts, all the little voices in my head telling me this man was dangerous. "Just tell me when you want me and I'll be there."

I was going to meet Blake Kildaire. It was one of my wildest dreams come true. And any girl in my position would have done exactly the same thing.

"I'm green with envy." Camilla was overwhelmed when I told her the next day. "I'll be your lady in waiting, anything, I'll polish your shoes. Just please let me meet my darling Blake."

Cam had Blake's autograph from when we'd gone to a major three-day event at Burnley. Ever since she had been obsessed with him and covered her bedroom with posters, and was saving up for a trip to the Horse of the Year Show. There had been a draw in *In the Saddle* to meet him and Cam had gone out and bought twenty copies to increase her chances.

"It's impossible," I said for the millionth time. "Monty insists, no friends."

Zoe was purposefully avoiding the yard and had even moved Lace to Jasper's for the rest of the summer holidays. Jade had gone off in a hired horsebox to fetch back Beachball who, the girl at Hyde Park said, refused to eat anything and was obviously pining.

Ash was furious with me for accepting Monty's offer and was clanging around the stables like a bull with a sore head. "Everybody can see he's a shark, so why can't you?" he bellowed when we were having one of umpteen rows.

"You're just jealous," I flung back. "I'm just doing this one job and you can't even be proud of me. What kind of a boyfriend are you?"

"One who cares about you and doesn't want to see you ripped off. Is that such a crime?"

"Well, I can look after myself," I pouted. "Just butt out, Ash, and concentrate on your own life."

We hadn't spoken to each other for the rest of the day.

I took Barney on a long hack and Cam tagged

along on The Hawk who was looking fantastic. Barney wasn't really walking out properly and every time I asked him to canter he hung back and just tried to trot faster. Camilla was wittering on about how when she got married she wanted to ride to church on a black stallion similar to the famous Downlands Cancarra.

"Shouldn't you concentrate on finding a man first?" I interrupted, irritably rubbing at my riding hat which was pressing into my temples. "You can't hang on to a bloke for more than five minutes."

She proceeded to tell me about Simon and how he was an ace kisser and she thought he was the "one" for her.

I had my mind too much on modelling to notice that Barney was continually edging onto the verges away from the hard roads.

We had a competition that weekend and Eric had high hopes that Barney was going to scorch away with the top prize. I hadn't told him yet about my assignment with Blake Kildaire. He was still steaming about the beach shoot and how I'd let Barney run riot through the village and leap into a goldfish pond.

It was so difficult to keep my mind both on modelling and on competing. I didn't know whether I was coming or going. Cam spent the rest of the hack knocking a show judge who was "obviously blind" and debating whether to invite Simon to the one-day event at the weekend. "The trouble is, he's so gorgeous I know everybody will be after him."

We clattered back into the yard, hot, sweaty and bothered and gasping for a cold drink. One of the livery owners who had a little Welsh Mountain pony was practising for a fancy dress class and her two little boys were bawling their eyes out covered from head to foot in plastic plant holders and trying their best to be Bill and Ben the flowerpot men.

Ash was lunging Dolly on the manege over some trotting poles and as soon as he saw me he brought her to a halt and gathered in the lunge rein. George, the big bay who was one of Ash's hopes for Burghley, was standing having his tail brushed by Judy and munching slowly on a trailing fuchsia. Ash once had to call the vet when he polished off a chunk of privet hedge which was meant to be a jump at a horse show and is actually poisonous to horses.

I put Barney in his stable and made a beeline for Ash who had taken Dolly inside and was unstrapping her roller and side reins. I couldn't bear not talking. It was driving me mad. I marched straight over to him and slipped my arms round his waist feeling the taut muscles in his stomach.

"I'm not letting go until you start talking to me."
I leant my head on his back.

"I never stopped talking to you," he grunted offhandedly. "You just don't like what I've got to say."

He slowly turned round letting me smother kisses all over his neck and chin. "Would you feel any better," I hugged him tighter, putting on my most seductive voice, "if you did some photo shoots too? Monty says you've got great potential."

He stiffened up immediately, pulling away as if I'd physically struck him. Dolly shot back, her beautiful dotted coat quivering as she picked up the tension.

"You just don't get it, do you?" Ash leered down at me looking as if he'd suddenly got a bad taste in his mouth. His voice was touched with acid. "I don't want anything to do with your stupid modelling. It's an empty, vacuous, vain, meaningless world to be in." He paused to catch his breath, looking down at me as if I was six years old. "You've changed, Alex. The girl I fell in love with lived and breathed horses. She had guts, ambition – she wasn't looking for an easy life."

"I'm not looking for an easy life." I nearly choked with indignation.

"Well I hope you enjoy it." He turned towards

the door, remote and impossible to reach. "But don't ever expect me to join in."

He stormed out, marching across to the house, his gorgeous legs clad in soft suede chaps and his blond hair curling sumptuously into the nape of his neck. I'd lost my heart to him and the thought of him not being there was as bad as losing an arm. But he couldn't tell me what to do. He couldn't always get his own way. I was entitled to my own life, my own interests.

But as I turned back to unclip Dolly's lead rope, I felt empty. I was setting off on a new chapter of my life and there was only one thing I really knew for sure. Ash was in no way part of it.

CHAPTER SIX

"Alex, have you pinched my curry comb?" Camilla was on the warpath and looking more competitive than I'd ever seen her. "Dad says if I win this competition he'll buy me a new CD player. Besides, Simon's coming and I want to impress him."

It was the morning of the one-day event and already things were starting to go wrong. Barney was being really obnoxious, picking up brushes with his teeth and throwing them across the stable, then sticking his head behind the hay net and refusing to come out. I'd lost my lucky pair of odd socks and my mum and dad had decided they'd turn up in the afternoon to watch.

It seemed really odd not having Zoe in the yard beavering away getting Lace immaculate, telling bad jokes and feeding us all with her various way-out snacks, like pea, cheese and egg sandwiches. It had only been a few days but I was missing her already.

Cam's mother arrived with their Range Rover and trailer and started lowering the ramp. I chased Nigel and Reggie out of Beachball's stable where they'd taken up residence.

We hadn't heard anything from Jade. She'd set off for Hyde Park in the hired horsebox, and had rung from a Little Chef to say she was all right. And nothing more. I'd even tried to find the telephone number of the livery stables but I couldn't remember the name. When I asked Monty he went off at the deep end and told me not to worry about Jade. He said she could look after herself and she had a record as long as your arm for being unreliable. Even so, it didn't add up.

Barney fidgeted while I bandaged his legs, being careful to keep an even pressure and tie the bow at the side rather than the front. I'd bought him a special poll guard to stop him hurting himself if he banged his head in the trailer and it made him look as if he'd got a Mohican hairstyle.

Cam loaded up The Hawk who was plunging around like a racehorse. Barney plodded out of his stable on stiff legs with a face like thunder. I was too busy pulling on gloves to protect my new manicure to give it any serious thought.

Ash was taking three four-year-olds he'd recently bought in for schooling and selling on. Judy was haring around loading them into the horsebox and piling up tack by the groom's door. She had black rings round her eyes from exhaustion. The black part-cob nicknamed Nobby lashed out with a cow kick which almost caught Judy full square on the knee.

Ash stalked across from the office not even noticing, barking instructions to get Red, a chestnut mare, ready first.

"What's eating him?" Cam was changing into her white shirt not caring that she was showing off a peach bra. Judy came across to us when Ash had disappeared, looking even worse close up.

"Umm, listen, you guys." She was holding on to Red who was nudging her impatiently in the chest, leaving green stains over her special "Jude knows best" T-Shirt. "I don't suppose either of you took any money from the office . . .?" Her voice trailed off guiltily.

Ash had a toby jug on the mantelpiece where he stuffed ten- and twenty-pound notes to be used for emergencies, the blacksmith and so on.

"The thing is, eighty quid's gone missing." Judy looked studiously at her feet. "When Ash finds out he's sure to blame me." She pushed back her bleached blonde hair which desperately needed the roots doing. "So if either of you know anything, anything at all . . ." Her eyes were pleading. Red snorted loudly with impatience. "I've been in trouble enough lately as it is. I really don't want to get the sack."

The showground was awash with people and horses with riders brick-red in the face and the collecting ring already a dust bowl. Mrs Brayfield, the Pony Club secretary, was sweating buckets and racing around with number cloths and score sheets. The loudspeaker was turned up extra loud and perforating everybody's ear drums.

Eric was over by the dressage arena, thundering out instructions and getting into an argument with someone's parents.

"Some things never change." Cam undid The Hawk's leg protectors.

I went for a burger and chips and caught a glimpse of Zoe tacking up Jasper's liver chestnut, Star. There was no sign of Lace, and Zoe was just in jeans. Typical of Jasper to get her working as his groom. He was probably off in the beer tent.

"Alex Johnson, what do you call that? A twenty metre circle or an egg?" Eric wasn't in the best of moods. "Maybe if you'd stop crimping your hair and do more riding you'd be a little more respectable." The hurt and disapproval in his eyes stood out a mile.

Just at the wrong moment a little girl with plaits and a massive ice cream came up and asked me if I was Cindy Crawford's sister.

Barney did terribly in the dressage. It was his worst score ever. He kept breaking into canter when he wasn't supposed to and hanging back when he was meant to go forward. Eric wheeled away in disgust. But for the first time ever I wasn't really bothered. Maybe I'd had enough of serpentines and leg yielding and transitions. Maybe there were other things in life and up until now I'd been too blinkered to see them.

By the time it got to walking the cross-country I was way down the scoreboard and Camilla was out in the lead. Eric left a note under the windscreen wiper of the Range Rover saying that if I wasn't bothered enough to try, he wasn't going to hang around wasting his time. He'd gone home and taken Daisy.

It wasn't my fault I wasn't doing well. How did he know I wasn't trying? All he ever did was shout the orders and criticize.

I stomped off to walk the course leaving Barney tied up in the trailer next to The Hawk. It was a simple enough course with some nice solid brush fences and not too many questions. The log pile in the wood was a little tricky, mainly because you had to turn on a sixpence and come at it from a few strides out. The secret would be to keep lots of impulsion, a nice bouncy stride.

Zoe was walking round with Jasper hand in hand. Cam was practically eating Simon, who had never seen a cross-country course before and was carrying on as if it was Badminton. They disappeared somewhere in the wood leaving me to plod around by myself feeling as if I'd got BO. Ash was doing the Horse Open Class and was still on his dressage, and even the Bevan brothers walked straight past me. Well, blow the lot of them.

"Would Alexandra Johnson please make her way to the refreshment tent. Thank you." It was Mrs Brayfield's voice over the tannoy. "That's urgently, please. Thank you."

Ash was already there when I arrived. Barney had tried to escape but had been caught just in time by an official.

Just as I was about to face the music, my mother appeared, totally unsuitably dressed, carrying my lucky socks.

"Oh there you are, dear. I thought you might like these!"

Barney moved forward towards the start of the cross-country, his ears twitching with anticipation. As usual, butterflies were swirling in my stomach and my brain was whirring. Cross-country is a bit like going on stage: you never lose that nervous feeling.

Jasper Carrington scorched back through the finish pumping the air with his fist. Barney half reared. The loudspeaker announced Camilla was still on the course and clear, going like the wind. I shortened my reins.

"Three. Two. One. *Go!* Good luck!"

We shot off towards the first fence in fifth

gear. "Steady, boy, steady." I leaned back slightly, ramming my feet in the stirrups.

The first fence was simple straw bales followed by a log pile and a hedge into a grass field. Barney was pounding along, taking a good hold. The wind whipped into my face and my chin strap came loose and started battering against my cheek. Barney was flying. We cleared a stone wall and turned downhill to another log, this time suspended off the ground so there was no ground line. I hated jumping downhill. I always felt out of control. Barney plunged and fought the bit trying to get his head down. The reins slid through my hands. "Steady, Barney. Wait!"

I hung on. He leapt forward half a stride, jumping far too big. I grabbed the martingale strap and felt him surge on. A sharp turn to the left and on to the bounce. Eric's words were etched so deeply in my brain I could hear him talking. It was like having a tape recorder in my pocket. "Hold him together, lots of impulsion. Don't let him jump too big."

We met the bounce just right. Barney pinged over, snapping up his forelegs and snaking over the second part. I was beginning to enjoy myself. I let Barney run on a little too much. He started breaking out in a sweat. That wasn't like Barney. He was super fit. He never sweated this early.

The next fence was a bank with a ditch in

front followed by a bounce to some small rails. We had to concentrate. Slowly, slowly. I found a good line. One, two, three. My legs were wrapped round him like a monkey on its mother's back. I was squeezing hard. But all of a sudden all the drive and attack drained out of him. I could feel him holding back. On the last stride he spooked at the ditch, half jumped and then swivelled to one side bolting under some trees.

"Barney!" I was more shocked than anything else. He never behaved like this.

He was yanking me under the low-lying branches so they were stinging my face and I couldn't see.

"Alexandra Johnson, first refusal at the bank. Camilla Davis home clear in the fastest time of the day."

I wasn't used to losing. I could sense that the whole showground was startled, straining to hear the commentary. Without thinking, I picked up the end of the reins and smacked them hard down on Barney's neck. He went berserk. He started running back, frantically heading for the fence steward's car.

"Hey, watch out!"

I managed to wheel him round in a tight circle and push him on again, driving with both heels. "Come on, Barney, don't be so stupid."

Guilt tore into me for hitting him. I never hit

Barney. He'd been abused enough before I got him. The bank was just a few strides away. I kept him steady and let him have a good look at the ditch. But it didn't do any good. As soon as we got to take-off he slithered back on his hocks, almost sitting down on the hard dusty ground. He wasn't going to jump. For the first time since Eric had taken over as trainer we risked being eliminated for three refusals.

I wrenched the reins tight and turned back for a final go. I could feel my cheeks burning bright pink and more and more people were stopping and crowding round. Please, Barney, you've got to jump this time.

My confidence was shredded. I went through the usual drill in my mind as I circled again. Heels down, shoulders back, legs on, look at the fence, keep straight, be determined.

But it was hopeless. Barney was a shaking, trembling mess.

"I think it's best to call it a day, love." The fence steward looked on pityingly as I slumped in the saddle.

I'd had enough. Somehow I'd have to ride back through the horseboxes and the crowds and face everybody.

Barney carted me the half mile back to the start, yanking at the reins until my arms were nearly dislodged from their sockets. I was fighting back tears and gritting my jaw so hard that I was nearly shattering my teeth. It was essential to be a good loser. I'd criticized Cam enough for throwing a wobbly in the past. It didn't matter. It was only a competition.

Barney seemed to calm down. Cam was the first person I saw, leading round The Hawk in a jazzy sweat rug, Simon hovering proudly in the background clutching four filthy brushing boots.

"Congratulations," I shouted and really meant it.

"Bad luck," she grinned back. "Anyway, there isn't any room in your house for more trophies."

We both knew that Cam had three times as many trophies as me and a whole wall of her bedroom covered in rosettes. But it was nice of her to say that.

Ash was waiting by the trailer looking sour faced and holding on to the chestnut mare, Red, who was plunging around determined to tie herself round the tow bar.

"Why didn't you take the alternative?" he hissed, glaring across at me from his near six-foot height. He was wearing his green and white colours with his stock undone slung round his neck.

"What alternative?" I stared blankly. When I walked the course I obviously hadn't noticed there was an easier route. Quite a few of the difficult fences had a simpler alternative for the less brave or inexperienced horses and riders. Knowing this just made me feel worse about the whole thing.

I dismounted, burying my head under the saddle flap, loosening the girth.

"Well, we can't all be as perfect as you," I snapped, rummaging in a pile of tack for the head collar.

Ash swung easily into the black jumping saddle his new sponsor had bought and reined the chestnut mare back between the two vehicles.

"And put the ramp up next time you leave him," Ash warned as a parting shot. "Next thing he'll be in the commentary caravan taking over the mike."

I stuck my tongue out at him and pulled off my body protector. Just at that moment I caught a glimpse through the wing mirror on the Range Rover and saw Jasper riding past on Star with Zoe clipping along at his side carrying bundles of rugs. She'd obviously been watching the whole scene with Ash. And most hurtful of all, worse than stuffing up on any cross-country course, she was smirking. Zoe Jackson was pleased that I'd done so badly. And it stung right to the very core.

CHAPTER SEVEN

Modelling was not all it was cracked up to be. It was boring and tedious and I was quietly having second thoughts. But there was no way Monty was going to let me slip through the net.

The next week was a whirlwind of photo shoots and unexpected meetings with various magazine editors which apparently were called go-sees. I'd never been so busy in my whole life. Barney had to be either put in the field or led out by Judy with another horse.

Monty was striking deals left, right and centre. Ash was becoming more and more distant and twice when I knocked on Eric's door he refused to answer, even though I could hear the television on inside and Daisy snuffling at the letter box.

The pictures of Barney at the beach were brilliant. They were taken in a kind of soft pinkish glow with the sea behind and Barney's yellow coat complementing the sand. *In the Saddle* had snapped them up for a front cover special and I had to do a quickie interview over the phone and talk about everything from my boyfriend to my favourite rider and my choice in mascara.

Monty promised the earth and like a fool I was stupid enough to listen. When I'd asked him if he'd heard from Jade he'd leapt up, almost knocking his desk flying. "Don't bother your pretty head about her. I'm the most important person in your life now." A small unpleasant smile slid over his face and then he backtracked, trying to be friendly. "You've got everything going for you; you're going to be rich and successful. Just concentrate on looking good and let me take care of the business."

But as yet I hadn't seen any money.

The only thing that kept me going was the thought of meeting Blake Kildaire. It was becoming an obsession. The morning of the photo shoot I was a bag of jittery nerves and my voice was so rattly I could hardly speak. The hired horsebox arrived at six o'clock in the morning to take Barney and myself up the A1. I'd already formulated a plan during the night – at four o'clock. Monty had told me what to do and like a fool I'd agreed to it – to leave Barney behind and take Dolly.

As the driver lowered the ramp and lit a cigarette I opened Dolly's door and led her purposefully up the ramp. I'd left a note in her manger for Ash explaining my reasons for kidnapping his best young horse. Barney stared over his door, puzzled, confused and rejected.

"Fifteen minutes, no longer." Someone banged on the caravan door.

In precisely a quarter of an hour I was going to meet Blake Kildaire and I didn't think my nerves could stand it. The make-up artist dabbed hectically at my nose and I reached for my third cup of coffee and crossed my legs to stop myself wanting the loo.

Outside was a first-class showjumping course where we were going to pose. We were at a showjumping yard in the depths of Yorkshire which belonged to a breeder who looked distinctly like Harvey Smith.

Blake's horse, Colorado, was being lunged on the arena and was like nothing I'd ever seen. He was half wild Mustang, half thoroughbred, from the plains of Colorado; a lovely skewbald. He had more charisma than Red Rum, Milton and Desert Orchid put together and was a dead cert for a gold medal at the next Olympics.

The girl lunging him was Mel from the horse and pony sanctuary Hollywell Stables. She was pretty and blonde and I'd read in umpteen magazines that she was Blake's closest friend. I'd been determined not to like her but she was so lovely and loved horses so much it was impossible.

"There, that will have to do." The make-up girl stood back and unclipped my protective gown. She had three earrings in each ear and a stud through her nose and had spent the last half an hour sneezing because she was allergic to horses. The make-up was so heavy that I felt as if my face had turned to cardboard. Apparently for photography you had to wear twice as much. I'd need a brillo pad to get rid of this lot.

I saw someone leading Dolly across the manege and joining the group of people standing by a blue and white triple bar. It was the same photographer but a sea of different faces. I was in full showjumping gear but instead of a black jacket I was wearing a special Horse Flair Wear quilted jacket.

Someone from *In the Saddle* with a clipboard and a goatee beard led me across to the group and pushed in towards the photographer. Suddenly I came slap bang against the rear view of the most fantastic pair of shoulders tapering into a solid back and long legs clad in Horse Flair Wear jodhpurs.

He turned round very slowly and steadily. And then I was staring into the most beautiful dark eyes I'd ever seen.

"Alex Johnson . . ." The photographer stepped forward. "I'd like you to meet Blake Kildaire."

He was absolutely gorgeous. When he shook my hand the warmth of his skin shot right up my arm. I couldn't take my eyes off him.

"Right, if we could have both horses and the two of you standing by this jump." The photographer fiddled with a tripod. Someone bounced up and rearranged my hair and then spent twice as long on Blake's.

A short bald man hovered near a car on the edge of the arena and the make-up girl whispered that he was the managing director from Horse Flair Wear. I saw Monty pull up in his BMW and smarm round him.

Dolly behaved impeccably for the first five minutes and then started backing up and jittering to each side. Her delicate flea-bitten grey coat became stained with sweat and her usually finely chiselled nostrils flared and snorted salmon pink. She felt like a spring about to explode.

"Just relax." The photographer dodged round for different angles. "Alex, you look too wooden. What's happened to that golden smile?"

The more I tried to relax, the harder it became. Dolly stood on my foot and twisted round. I was trying to prop myself up on a showjump pole but my legs wouldn't go in the right place. Blake winked at me from on top of Colorado. He looked like a mega-star.

The guy with the goatee beard was chatting

up the make-up artist who was apparently called Happy. "Oh, if only I could feel Happy," he kept babbling until the photographer snapped his head off and threw a reel of film at him. Dolly shot back, clipping her hocks on the poles and demolishing the jump in three seconds. The whole set had to be built up again.

"Where's the yellow horse?" The managing director moved forward, with Monty running at his heels. "This mare is too pretty, too bland." His German accent was very distinctive. "You don't look relaxed with her." He stared at me with X-ray eyes. "The other horse had charisma – he looked – how do I say, unusual."

"But . . . but I thought . . ." The whole session was turning into a nightmare. I'd blushed brick red and could feel perspiration breaking out on my top lip.

From there it just got worse. Dolly became more and more nervous and Monty kept shooting me angry looks. Then it started to rain. Blake was a perfect gentleman. He came with me to have a cup of tea and insisted on giving me his jacket. I asked for his autograph and he promised to send me a signed sweatshirt.

"You're so good at this, so natural," I moaned, feeling like a square peg in a round hole.

"Are you joking?" He looked down at me with a tenderness which warmed my bones. "I'm only doing this to raise money for Hollywell Stables. I hate every minute of it. It reminds me of school photographs."

"Really?" I suddenly felt a great weight lifting off my shoulders.

I couldn't ignore what was going on in my heart. I'd thrown myself into modelling because I was running away from eventing. I was scared I wasn't going to make the grade and it was better to give up than to face up to failure. I was being a coward and I'd lost all my friends; Zoe, Ash and most of all Eric and Barney. I'd been a misguided fool and now I was stuck with a battleaxe of a manager and a job which was hard work and boring and no fun at all. What's more, I hadn't been paid.

"A word of advice, Alex." Blake pressed my arm exquisitely gently so I broke out in goose pimples. "Go back to eventing. Follow your heart. If you don't you'll regret it for the rest of your life."

"But . . . but how do you know?" I could feel my bottom lip starting to tremble.

"I just do, OK. You're a class rider. Eric Burgess has one of the best eyes in the country. You've got to trust him."

"But how do you know about Eric?" I was confused now. I couldn't understand how Blake knew so much.

Then he pulled out a white envelope from his coat pocket with scrawly spidery handwriting on the front. "Let's just say Eric filled me in."

"He wrote to you?" I was stunned.

"He's a wily character." Blake smiled down at me so I felt a surge of new strength. "He knew if you were going to listen to anyone it would be me." He grinned mischievously. "I think he called it hero worship."

"Oh." I stared down into my cold scummy tea, reeling in embarrassment.

"He cares about you, Alex, very much. Sometimes people don't always show it. Do yourself a favour. Grasp the nettle, chase after what's really in your heart. Before it's too late."

"Hold her steady!" Kit the Nit, the photographer, was getting more and more irate as Dolly plunged around swaying her quarters into every possible obstruction.

The managing director of Horse Flair Wear was starting to glower and Monty was hopping around as wet and slippery as a fish, intent on pulling off some sort of deal.

Dolly had finally had enough. When the photographer flew into a tantrum and started waving his arms in the air like a maniac she backed away and crashed heavily into a pile of poles.

"Dolly, whoa, whoa, it's all right!" Luckily I

was on the ground but I couldn't hold on to the lead rope any longer and she went careering off towards the end of the manege. Blake was at my side in a shot.

"Never mind the ruddy horse," Kit squawked. "Look at my best camera!"

Blake was incredible. He edged over to Dolly who was screwed up in the corner, shaking, sweat pouring off her. Very quietly he whispered to her and made strange clucking noises and then blew into her nostrils and rubbed her ears. Within seconds she quietened and let him take hold of the trailing lead rope. "It's all right, girl, nobody's going to hurt you . . ."

"I want the yellow horse." The MD from Horse Flair Wear was emphatic. Monty's eyes were greedy and gloating. I was trying to hide a huge rip in the expensive tartan coat I was wearing. Suddenly I looked up, being skewered by stares from every side. I couldn't believe what he was asking. "That horse has the charm, the interest, I want to hire him."

"I'll get a contract drawn up straight away." Monty rubbed his hands together.

The words seeped into my brain but it was a few moments before they lodged there. It was Monty's fleshy lips quivering with excitement which snapped me out of a trance.

"Well?" The MD twitched with his glasses.

Very methodically I peeled off the tartan coat and then crumpled it into a missile and hurled it full on at Monty. "You can stuff your crummy contract and your modelling and all your false promises." I was livid. "Last week you were calling him an old nag and now you smell profit you're talking about him like one of the Queen's corgis. You make me sick."

Monty's eyes hardened to bullets and his mouth snapped shut. "You can't talk to me like that. You're under contract."

"I'm not under contract. I'm going home."

"I wouldn't do that if I were you, young lady." His voice was heavily laced with threat.

"I think the young lady has made herself very clear." Blake stepped in, towering over them both, quietly making a point. "I think she's had enough."

I took Dolly's lead rope off Blake and marched over to the hired horsebox. "If you're quitting, you'll have to walk home. I'm not paying you." Monty curled his lip at me.

"Then she'll come with me." Blake came and put a steady hand on my shoulder. He was fantastic, just like a hero from Barbara Cartland. "I think your modelling days are over, don't you?"

Going home in Blake's ultra-modern HGV horsebox with Colorado and Dolly in the back was like a hazy dream. If Cam knew she wouldn't talk to me for the rest of her life. I had Blake entirely to myself in the cab because Mel had gone back to Hollywell Stables with her family.

I decided that he had a boyish grin like Mel Gibson but an intensity and charisma like Heathcliff. We were studying Wuthering Heights in English and I knew I'd never be able to read it the same way again. I tried not to let my eyes linger on the powerful shoulders clearly defined through his white shirt. Instead I talked intelligently about showjumping and related distances and fished for gossip on the Whitaker brothers and Nick Skelton.

As we pulled through the main gates of the Burgess estate I suddenly remembered that I had Ash's pride and joy in the back, who I had kidnapped. He was most likely strutting up and down in the common room plotting to assassinate me.

The hairs on the back of my neck suddenly prickled to nervous attention. George was hanging his head over the door, resting his chin on the metal strip with his bottom lip hanging open and his ears flopped apart.

Barney raced to the door and started neighing his head off; then he seemed to remember that he'd been left behind and his face became sad.

There was no sign of Ash.

I climbed out of the cab and Blake followed me into the common room. Everything was as normal apart from Judy crumpled in a heap with her head in her arms bawling her eyes out. She looked up, mascara streaking in black rivulets down her cheeks, and gaped at Blake. Her swollen eyelids flew open in shock.

"Jude, what is it? What's happened?" She couldn't register anything but Blake. I felt like shaking her shoulders.

Blake immediately moved forward offering a big white starched hanky. Judy blew her nose like a bugle and then blinked at Blake as if having a dry nose would suddenly make him disappear.

"Judy – where's Ash?"

She dragged her eyes away from Blake and they watered up all over again. "He's given me the sack," she bawled. "He thinks I'm a thief." She collapsed in heaving sobs.

"Don't cry, Judy, we'll sort this out. Where's Ash?"

She stared at me uncomprehending and then the blanket of fog lifted and she gulped and strained to find her voice.

"Jade rang. She's in trouble. Apparently she's at a transport café on the motorway out of Blackpool. She's got Beachball with her. They're stranded in the car park . . ."

CHAPTER EIGHT

Beachball's lovely black and white splodgy head poked over the partition in the horsebox with hay trailing all round his ears.

"Isn't he gorgeous?" Jade stood by the ramp quivering with hunger and exhaustion, looking as if she'd shed pounds. "It's all right, darling, you're safe now."

Ash led him out, taking care not to rush him, watching his bad foreleg which was all bandaged up from knee to fetlock. He'd had loads of stitches and was on painkillers and antibiotics.

Barney let out an ear-piercing neigh as soon as he caught sight of his new friend. Even Nigel and Reggie quacked and shuffled their wings and refused to move out of the way. Beachball was put in a stable next to Barney. It's important when a horse has had a shock to keep everything as familiar as possible. Jack Douglas, our vet, was filling up a syringe with a tetanus vaccination. Beachball hardly noticed as he jabbed the needle into his neck and within seconds it was all over. Ash bolted the stable door and went to make up a nice warming bran mash.

I put my arm in Jade's and coaxed her back to the common room where she had a little cry and I finally managed to persuade her to have a cup of tea and half a Mars bar for energy.

Camilla came in and put an arm round Jade and then Judy brought in Beachball's bandages and said Jack Douglas had just left and Beachball was going to be fine.

It was only when everybody else had left, three cups of tea later, that Jade clenched her hands together and started to tell Ash and myself the whole gory story.

She'd arrived at Hyde Park in the hired horsebox to find that Beachball wasn't there. They'd said that Mr Brentford had contacted them that morning and Beachball had been taken away a few hours earlier. She'd rung Monty from a payphone and in a fit of temper he'd admitted that "the nag" was back where he belonged. That could only mean Blackpool on the Golden Mile. I drew in my breath sharply when I realized what she meant.

"The pig sold him back to his previous owner." Jade was trembling, wringing her hands together so the knuckles whitened. "How could he do that? He knows how much I love Beachball. He's the only person I've got in my whole life."

She stood up. "I didn't have enough money for diesel for the lorry so I set off hitchhiking and managed to thumb a lift with a lorry driver and then a family with two kids."

My chest tightened at the thought of a girl like Jade thumbing a lift alone. It was so dangerous – she shouldn't have done it under any circumstances.

"I arrived in Blackpool exhausted, as you can imagine, and I walked up and down the sea front for three hours without seeing a thing. I started to think I'd got it wrong. Blackpool was full of donkeys and horses but none of them Beachball." She sat down again, a bundle of quivering nerves.

I remembered Jade telling me about Blackpool's Golden Mile. A long road along the sea front bursting with arcades, fast food places, nightclubs, litter.

"I couldn't go home." Jade started up again. "I had to give it another day." She hesitated and then went on. "I had five pounds on me. I bought two stale doughnuts and slept the night on the beach."

We all fell silent. Ash's eyebrows were furrowing into ruts. "But . . ." He ran a hand through his hair in embarrassment. "But you must be loaded – you've been at the top for years. What about credit cards?"

Jade let a thin small smile pass over her face. "Don't you mean Monty's credit cards? He controls everything. I don't even have my own bank account. I'm penniless."

I was so shocked I could have fallen backwards. Ash froze.

"I trusted Monty. He was more like a dad in the early days. All I was interested in was fame and adoration. As long as he gave me enough money for what I wanted I was happy. I never knew how much I was earning. I didn't care. Not until six months ago. I found some papers Monty had left out. He's been ripping me off for years."

Long moments ticked past with Jade sitting staring at her nails.

"Go on," Ash urged, impatient. I gave him a look but Jade started to talk.

"I didn't spot Beachball until the middle of the next afternoon. He was in a buggy in a traffic queue that wasn't moving, pinned in between a Ford Escort full of yobbos and an ice cream van behind. My poor baby's nose was pressed against the Escort's back windscreen. I went berserk. He was with the same man I'd bought him off originally. He recognized me and demanded a thousand pounds. His eyes were dripping in greed. He made me sick."

"So what did you do?" I was on the edge of my seat with tension. I expected her to say she fetched the police.

"I sat on a bench and tried to work out how

to raise the money. I was just about to give up when the accident happened. The idiots in the Ford Escort reversed into Beachball, which is how he hurt his leg. Then it turned out the miserable lout who was working him didn't have a licence and he panicked when someone went to ring the police. He legged it, leaving Beachball with me."

"Wow." I shook my head in disbelief.

"A vet came out and organized a lift with a breeder as far as Leeds. That's when I rang Ash. I was stuck in a car park in a transport café on the M62."

I mindlessly made another cup of tea and added three teaspoons of salt.

"I haven't had a chance to tell you." Jade rubbed a hand over her face, pulling her hair over one shoulder. "I hope you can forgive me. I took eighty pounds out of a toby jug in your office. I always meant to pay it back. I only borrowed it."

"Oh." Ash didn't say a word about Judy losing her job. He just silently went out of the door, across the yard to where his ex-head groom was packing her things in the tack room. For one of the rare occasions in Ash's life he was going to have to go down on his knees and admit he was wrong. I only hoped Judy made him squirm.

Three hours later we were standing outside the Wellington hotel where Monty was supposed to be checking out the next morning and heading back to London – with Jade.

I was wearing my best jeans and shirt and the black leather jacket which I'd posed in on the beach. Jade looked thin, tired, but with enough spirit to go through with the plan. Ash had dropped us off a couple of streets away and now it was down to us.

Jade squeezed my hand and we crossed the road trying to be brave. Jade had admitted to Ash and myself that she had encouraged me to be a model for her own ends. Monty had promised that if she got me to sign up she could have six months off doing whatever she wanted. No more New York, no more catwalk or glossy magazines. She'd been desperate enough to accept.

We went up in the lift to the sixth floor. He knew we were coming. Jade had rung him up earlier and organized a meeting. I'd expected her to shout and scream but her voice had been stripped of emotion, just icy cold. She meant business.

A tall redhead aged about nineteen was coming out of room 201 wearing a big smile and carrying a portfolio. Another one to be sucked in by the Monty charm.

Jade tapped on the door. I heard Monty's oily voice say "Enter" and she flung the door back on its hinges.

"Jade, darling, lovely to see you." Monty was sitting behind a desk which he'd moved into the middle of the room twiddling leisurely with a biro, his teeth flashing dangerously in false bonhomie.

Jade lifted a hand up to her baseball cap and pulled it back, but there was no flowing mane of ice-blonde hair. Instead there was a neat bob of dark brown hair cropped into her neck with a spiky fringe. It made her look boyish and gaunt, her huge eyes standing out even with no make-up.

Monty's eyebrows flew up in alarm.

"No more Jade Lamond," she sneered, looking for strength and finding it. "I'm not the new Claudia Schiffer. I never was and I never will be. I'm plain Helen Taylor."

"I presume . . ." Monty carefully laid down the pen. "I presume this is rebellion because I disposed of that stupid horse. Well, let me tell you, dear, I did you a favour. If you like, I'll buy you a goldfish. Or what about a poodle?"

Jade quietly smiled and folded her arms. "I despise you, Monty Brentford, and I'm going to expose you to the whole world."

Monty momentarily lost his composure, doubt flickering in his eyes. Then the sickly charm was back in place, a mask of false caring, and he was asking her what she could possibly mean. He'd booked her in for a holiday in Florida, she could take anyone she liked, stay as long as she wanted. It was his treat.

Jade tutted and stepped forward. "I believe you owe my friend some money." She was so cool it was brilliant.

Monty was getting fed up.

"She's got a load of riding gear from it – what more does she want? The stupid girl had her chance and she threw it away."

Jade didn't back off.

"I want you to write a cheque out for Alex and I want you to hand over my contract."

Monty laughed out loud.

"I mean it, Monty. I'm not messing about."

"I'm sure you're not, dear. You've never had the brains to be anything but honest."

"If you don't agree to my requests I shall be telling my life story to the *News of the World* and the *New York Times*. The choice is yours." Jade stood up to her full height and jutted out her chin. "I'll be in their London office tomorrow morning."

"Don't you dare threaten me, girl." Monty leapt up, almost crashing over the table. "I'll have your guts for garters if you start that game."

"I'm sure they'll be interested to know how you used to lock me in my room if I refused to work. How you used to force me to take laxatives to keep slim. How all my money is in an overseas account in your name."

Monty was scarlet with rage. His jaw kept falling open and snapping shut. He looked as if he was going to explode with anger. When he did speak his voice was thick and harsh. "You wouldn't do that to me. You were nothing when you met me. I made you. And you've got no proof anyway." He slouched back against the desk.

I was frightened now. He looked capable of anything. Jade took a step back. Monty grabbed a heavy granite paperweight from the desk and waved it threateningly in the air. "Any more talk like that," his eyes had narrowed to thin slits, "and I'll squash you. You're finished anyway – Claudia could wipe the floor with you." His mottled hand shook uncontrollably.

Suddenly the door burst open and Ash thundered into the room, knocking Monty flying back against the desk and twisting his arm behind his back. The paperweight crashed to the floor.

Jade ran towards a black briefcase in the corner and fiddled with the combination lock.

"You're a bully boy, do you know that?" Ash pressed all his bulk against Monty. "There ought to be a law against people like you . . . You make me sick."

"I've got it!" Jade held up a thick wad of paper. "It's the original. He always carries it in his briefcase."

"I've got copies," Monty gasped, turning purple.

"This won't stand up in court." Jade waved it at him, victorious. "You can't frighten me any more, Brentford. You're pathetic."

She brought across his cheque book and made him write out a cheque with Ash still holding his left arm.

"You can't get away with this," he growled. "It's not legal."

"Oh shut up and just do it, you greedy, mean little man." Jade wasn't frightened of him any more – it shone out from every nerve in her body. Ash took the cheque and released his vice-like grip. Monty stood rubbing his arm like a petulant child.

"I'm not going to the newspapers." Jade stood in the doorway, looking back at him with disgust. "I never want to see you again, Monty. I'm going to start a new life."

Monty was about to speak but she raised her hand and stopped him before he got out a single word.

"You'll be having a visitor tomorrow, from the Serious Fraud Squad. I photocopied some of your papers a few months ago and I think they'll be very interested to know why you haven't been paying tax on undeclared income for the last ten years."

Monty staggered back as if he'd been hit hard.

"I had to do it, Monty." Jade weakened ever so slightly. "You've ruined too many people's lives. Somebody had to stop you."

The door clicked shut and we all stood in the corridor, emotionally battered, trying to recover from the ordeal.

Then a huge, warm, all-engulfing grin spread across Jade's face, lighting up her perfect features. "Do you realize," she put an arm round each of us, "this is the first time since my fourteenth birthday that I feel . . ." She struggled for the word, tears welling up in her eyes and her bottom lip trembling. "Free!"

Barney stood in his stable with a face as sour as vinegar and his hindquarters turned towards the door in no uncertain terms.

"Barney, please talk to me." I'd offered him sliced apples, carrots, a swede which had dropped off a tractor and endless chocolates and mints. But there was no way he was going to be bribed.

"Barney, it's you I love. I adore you. Can't you at least try to forgive me?"

He snatched at a mouthful of hay and scowled.

I sat down in the clean straw I'd just banked up round the sides and pulled out Monty's cheque.

It read £850. It was more than I'd ever seen in my life. I ran my finger over the black ink and swirly signature and made a very difficult decision. Ash popped his head over the stable door clutching a box of Belgian chocolates, a present from Jade.

"A penny for your thoughts," he grinned.

I passed him the cheque which he held between thumb and forefinger, squinting in the dim light. "So is the dressage saddle on order or haven't you decided the colour yet?"

His eyes twinkled with mischief.

"Neither," I said with no regrets. "I'm donating the whole lot to Hollywell Stables."

Ash didn't say a word. I stood up, walked across and planted my arms round his neck looking forward to a big cuddle. "I don't want to be reminded of Monty," I explained. "Every time I put the saddle on Barney he'd be there like a nagging sore tooth."

Ash bent down and kissed my forehead and my eyelids.

"Hollywell Stables needs it more than me, and if it helps save a horse's life then some good will have come from it."

"Good lass," said Ash, his perfect seductive mouth hovering near mine. "For a minute back there I thought you were turning into a snotty-nosed primadonna."

Barney came up behind me and booted me in the back, snuffling in my pocket.

"So we're talking again, are we?" I threw my

arms round his neck and gave him a sloppy kiss on the nose. "It took you long enough!"

"That horse is continually interfering in my love life." Ash pushed away Barney's nose and nibbled my neck.

"But he is the best horse in the world." I turned back to Barney.

"All you've got to do now," Ash opened the door for me, "is win over Eric."

Somehow I didn't think that was going to be quite so easy.

CHAPTER NINE

"Come on, Eric," I muttered. "A girl could die out here."

"Five minutes!" The front door clattered open and Eric yelled at the top of his voice. "You're infuriating and stubborn."

"That makes two of us," I yelled back, bolting for the door, as the heavens opened with another thunderous downpour.

The cottage was warm and well lit and Daisy went mad when she saw me in the doorway. Her stubby paws scratched against my legs as she tried to lick my face, wag her tail and bark at the same time. I gave her a hug and she flung herself into my shoulder.

"All right, calm down, calm down. She hasn't been gone that long." Eric wheeled back to the coffee table where he'd obviously been podding peas and watching EastEnders. "I thought you only watched documentaries." I watched his discomfort as I caught him out.

"I do," he barked. "I'm waiting for Tomorrow's World."

Daisy jumped up onto the settee and

slobbered all down the armrest. I hadn't realized how much I'd missed her.

"Glad to see you haven't got all that muck on your face." He tried to look blasé, but peas were shooting all over the carpet. "Ash told me about that Brentford character."

"I suppose you're going to say 'I told you so'."

"I'm sure you've learnt your lesson."

"Oh thanks." I was starting to feel really uncomfortable. He hadn't mentioned Barney.

"Would you like a chocolate biscuit?" Eric bundled off into the kitchen to make a pot of tea and came back with the biscuits on a china plate.

I started eating a biscuit, but I couldn't wait any longer. Spitting crumbs all over my knee I launched straight in at the deep end, my voice croaking with passion and remorse.

"I've been such a fool," I bawled. "I just want everything back to normal. I can't bear not having you as my trainer. It's eventing I want to do, not modelling. You've got to believe me, you've got to."

Eric whipped out a starchy white hanky. "Here, blow your nose and have another chocolate biscuit."

"Well?" I blew my nose and stared at him with sad limpid eyes.

Eric kept me in suspense for another five

minutes while he fiddled with the peas, trying to make room for them in the fridge.

"Eric!" I felt like strangling him.

"I'm only going to be your trainer if you buckle down. No more poncing around in front of a camera – I want total commitment."

"Yes, yes," I begged. I'd agree to doing a bungee jump if it made things better.

"No more slacking off, not concentrating or criticizing Barney. That horse is as good as you ride him."

"Yes, anything." I pummelled a coffee-coloured cushion and pleated the edges.

"You've got a lot of catching up to do."

"I'll send off some entry forms straight away."

"No need." Eric rustled behind his back and pulled out a schedule. "I've already booked you into Redbourne. I knew you'd come to your senses – eventually."

He scowled at me and propped a pair of glasses on his nose. "Now you're going to have to get your act together for this course – it's the hardest you've ever tackled. Oh and by the way, those chocolate biscuits . . ."

He gave me a wicked smile. "I opened the wrong packet – they're Daisy's."

Chocolate-flavoured Bonio suddenly tasted like chaff in my mouth as I choked until my eyes watered and threw the cushion at Eric who was having hysterics.

"What does this mean, a wet nose and a shiny coat?"

"Come on." Eric threw my coat at me and moved towards the begonia plant pot for his car keys. "We must have a look at Barney. There's something wrong with his feet. I'd bet my life on it."

Barney held up his near foreleg, delighted that Eric was in his stable showing him so much attention. Daisy sat in the corner chewing on a dandy brush. I supported Barney's leg while Eric jabbed around the cleft of the frog with a penknife and shining a torch.

"Well?" I was on tenterhooks. There's an old adage, "No foot, no 'oss", and if something was wrong with Barney's feet, just supposing . . .

"Corns." Eric leaned back flashing the torch-light in my face. "Just as I thought."

"Corns? I thought that's what old people got?"

"Tut." Eric levered his wheelchair round to the other side. "Honestly, Alex, sometimes your equine knowledge is severely lacking. Now come here and hold up this leg."

I did as I was told.

"Now look there, can you see that pink

spot?" Eric had cut away at some of the dead sole and even I could see the throbbing red mark.

"We've caught it early enough." Eric sounded relieved. "Even the great old Desert Orchid used to have corns so I wouldn't say you're on the scrap heap yet." He slapped Barney's shoulder affectionately. "All we've got to do now is get the blacksmith."

"But, Eric." I tried to reason with him. "It's ten o'clock at night!"

The blacksmith readjusted his suede protective chaps, grunted and picked up Barney's off-foreleg brandishing a rasp.

The Calor gas cylinder was on full blast warming up a three quarter length shoe which Eric had insisted on. The local radio station's golden oldie classics were drifting out from the blacksmith's van and Daisy suddenly came to life searching for bits of hoof which dogs love and are supposed to be full of vitamins. I offered the blacksmith a cup of Thermos stewed tea. How Eric had persuaded him to come out at eleven o'clock at night I really didn't know. I'm sure he must have concocted some far-fetched story.

The blacksmith, who was built like Giant Haystacks, held Barney's hoof as tenderly as a thrush's egg. He explained how he had to relieve the pressure on the seat of the corn for it to heal.

Once he'd got an audience there was no stopping him. The corns were really bruises and had probably been caused from the hard ground or a bad landing after a jump.

No wonder the poor little baby had refused three times at the bank complex. He must have been in real pain. Guilt gnawed at my insides that I hadn't worked it out for myself. What kind of horse owner was I?

Eric had mixed up a poultice in an old sack which he was going to pull onto Barney's worst hoof. It smelt awful. He refused to tell either of us what was in it and I pitied Barney for having to put up with the smell all night long. Daisy had long since fled into the common room.

"Right." Eric left Barney to it and closed his door. I expected Barney to have a week or so's rest as that was the usual procedure and what the blacksmith had suggested before he left.

"I'll see you at six o'clock in the morning." Eric gave me an encouraging smile. "We're going to the beach."

It turned out to be a real knees-up. Camilla came along with The Hawk and had a quick gallop and spent the rest of the time sunbathing. We hadn't actually started off until mid-morning. Ash brought Dolly who thoroughly enjoyed the experience and kept carting Ash into the sea. I had to paddle Barney up and down for an hour and a half and got absolutely drenched. Eric had no sympathy when I slipped and went splashing into the water head first. Barney nuzzled my hair and then tried to roll in the wet sand. The fun really started when Daisy decided she wanted a paddle too and kept doing doggy shakes all over Eric.

The temperature was soaring. Ash took over holding Barney in the sea, the whole idea being that the salt water would reduce the bruising. Eric planned to do this every day for the next two weeks and then set up a canter training programme on the sands.

Camilla was stretched out on a horse blanket putting Ambre Solaire between her toes which I really thought was taking it too far. Every few minutes she looked up with the hope of spotting some talent but the only people on the beach were a few old-age pensioners and mothers with their toddlers.

"Now tell me all over again, what was Blake like, did you fancy him, and is that Mel his girl-friend, officially? Do you think I've got any chance? Even the remotest sliver?"

I was just wondering what had happened to the sultry Simon when she said something which made my ears stick out like radar.

"By the way, Zoe's split up with Jasper. Toukie's come back from America and Jasper ran after her like a lovesick puppy with his tail between his legs. Zoe's devastated and won't answer the phone or come out of the house."

"Why didn't you tell me this earlier?" I leapt up, kicking sand all over Cam's bare midriff.

"Well you've hardly been around to tell, have you, what with all this modelling. Anyway," Cam pulled a face, "it only happened two days ago. Zoe made me promise not to tell you."

I sat on Zoe's neat front lawn with my legs crossed waiting to see the curtains twitch. If necessary I'd sit there all day. She couldn't shut herself away. It wasn't healthy and it wasn't necessary. We'd all been sucked into situations which were not all they seemed, and if I could get over them then so could Zoe. Life was too short.

She opened the door five minutes later looking bug-eyed and scruffy with Garfield slippers on her feet and her hair unbrushed and probably unwashed. "So Cam told you?" Her voice was barely more than a whisper. "I thought she would."

I followed her into the kitchen. There were two empty cola bottles on the table, surrounded by Quality Street wrappers.

"Somebody's been having a major chill-out." I wrinkled up my nose at something in the oven which smelt like burnt bacon.

"Well, there's no need to look down your

nose," Zoe snapped and then put a hand over her face. "I'm sorry. I heard about Monty – it seems we've both been taken in."

She slumped into an armchair and flicked off the telly which was cartoon time with Bugs Bunny.

I started to pour out my heart. I covered everything, not missing out a single detail and when I had finished Zoe was crying, tears running down her cheeks.

"I was jealous of you, do you know that? My best friend. I was sick of you always being so perfect, so good at everything. What kind of a friend does that make me, to feel like that?"

"Perfectly normal, I should say." I moved across and put my arm round her sagging shoulders and squeezed her. "I can be a bit bolshy at times. I should think I deserved it. But I've certainly got my feet on the ground now."

"Oh Alex, why do I always fall for the wrong men? First Jack Landers, then Jasper. I'm sick of getting hurt."

She clung to me and I reached into my pocket and pulled out Eric's hanky. "Here, blow your nose and have another chocolate."

A wry smile flickered on my face and I tweaked her nose and helped myself to a toffee. I'd got back my best friend. Everything was fitting into place. "You'll meet the right guy, I promise you, eventually. Anyway . . ." I paused while I

101

extricated the toffee from a back molar. "At fifteen you're hardly over the hill, are you?"

I coaxed her into coming back to the yard for some toffee pecan ice cream which I'd seen Ash sneak into the common room fridge. We decided that Ash and I would fetch Lace back from Jasper's that afternoon.

When we arrived, Cam was flitting around the garden at the side of the manege in a bikini getting Jenny to take a photograph.

"You're not quick enough," Cam protested, after she'd been posing with gritted teeth for long minutes. Then she noticed the washing line in the background with a whole set of brushing boots strung up and two pairs of Ash's boxer shorts. "Oh that's really going to make a good impression, isn't it?"

"This time you're really going to kill her." Judy came out of the common room with a damp envelope addressed to me and with the Hollywell Stables stamp in the corner. "She steamed it open – can you believe it? I'd string her up next to those boxer shorts if I was you."

I quickly scanned the letter which was from Blake thanking me on behalf of Hollywell Stables for my generous donation and suggesting that he came down to do a free lecture/demonstration for the Sutton Vale Pony Club. It was a marvellous offer.

"Now she's prancing around trying to get a decent picture which she's going to send to him. He'll think she's one of those demented crackpot fans." Judy was glaring scornfully at Cam who had snatched the camera from Jenny and was trying to work the automatic timer.

All I could do was burst into a fit of giggles. I told them I wasn't a bit bothered about the steamed letter and the invasion of privacy. Judy and Zoe stared at me as if I'd turned into Mother Teresa. "Don't you see?" I grinned. "As long as I'm not in the frame I don't care!"

CHAPTER TEN

Jade stayed on at the stables for another couple of weeks until she got herself sorted out on a course to become a veterinary nurse. And then she moved Beachball to be closer to her and sent us regular photographs of her dissecting dead rats or practising giving injections into Jaffa oranges and looking after an assortment of cats and dogs. She was bursting with happiness and said she'd found her true vocation. Monty was picked up at Heathrow airport the morning after our visit. He'd been trying to skip the country and was now undergoing a massive investigation into his business affairs.

Barney was going from strength to strength and his feet very soon became a corn-free zone. The sea had worked wonders and now we were getting him fit on the beach where the sand was soft enough to avoid any jarring.

I spent hours sitting in his stable on an upturned bucket, telling him he was special, building up his confidence, and even reading to him out loud. His favourite books were mysteries or anything to do with horses. Ash said I'd lost my marbles but we were a team again and that's what mattered.

Eric was back on form, bellowing out instructions and writing out training programmes, sitting on the beach in his wheelchair, drinking a flask of tea and shouting at me continually to keep up Barney's head, to gallop in a rhythm. "Never underestimate the importance of rhythm."

Zoe said he was like a broken record and my mother knitted him a multicoloured scarf which he wore with pride even though it trailed round his wheels and scared the horses to death.

Redbourne was drawing closer and closer. It was a major competition covered by all the horse magazines and one where junior selectors were hovering around by every tree.

Barney was having roughly two hours' exercise a day, made up of hacking, canter work, schooling, lunging and jumping. Eric had me jogging two miles a day and lifting dumbells fifty times to build up my shoulders. Zoe nicknamed me Rocky Balboa, and Barney the Italian Stallion, but I drew a line at drinking raw eggs for breakfast.

I was determined to win back my spurs. The pressure was really on. Eric was working like crazy on the dressage and showjumping. "Think of the cross-country as the bread and butter and the dressage and showjumping as the icing on the cake. That's where you make up the winning points."

It was drilled into me that the word dressage comes from the French verb *dresser* and means training and deportment. "At the moment you both carry yourselves like sacks of potatoes."

Eric was spending hours on cantering over poles on the ground and cavaletti, concentrating on the corners and the approach. At one stage I blew up and demanded that we did some proper jumping instead of poncing around like riding school beginners.

Eric turned red and blasted me out. "Have you ever thought that a showjumping round is dressage interrupted by fences?"

I stared at him blankly. The next morning there was a letter propped up in the common room waiting for me: "In a round of, say, two minutes you might spend seven to nine seconds in the air, the rest of the time is spent getting to the fences and making a good getaway. If you arrive at a fence well and leave it well, the jump is bound to be good. THINK ON!"

I didn't argue again.

Ten days before the competition we loaded up and went to a cross-country practice ten miles away where there were natural banks, ditches, water and a variety of complexes involving bounces and tight turns. Eric made me memorize a course and Barney soared over everything as fast as a well-tuned Ferrari. When we pulled up by

Eric my stopwatch recorded four minutes thirty seconds and Barney was barely puffing.

Eric nodded his head, and smiled up at us, tapping his fingers excitedly on the armrest of his chair. "He's ready!"

"I'm not ready!" I bawled, pulling my back protector on over my cross-country shirt and grabbing Ash's arm in a vice-like grip. "I can't remember," I shrieked, "after fence nine, where do I turn?"

"Alex, calm down, think it all out." Ash wrapped his arms round me but could only feel the polystyrene wall of my new back protector. Underneath my heart was hammering ten to the dozen. "Take one fence at a time and it will all come back."

I'd walked the course four times but I was still frightened to death of forgetting my way. I'd analysed every fence, made copious notes, logged every alternative, but I still didn't have my usual confidence.

Outside Cam and Zoe were tacking up Barney as if it was some kind of ritual. Grackle noseband, breastplate, surcingle, leg grease, bootlace attached from the bridle to the first plait. Jumping whip. Boots.

I'd completed the dressage and the showjumping and we were lying in the lead. I didn't know anybody else at the competition but the standard was red-hot. I was riding for my life. Zoe led Barney round with a rug thrown over his quarters. Ash made me eat half a Kit-Kat for energy.

Eric suddenly appeared from behind a cream horsebox looking concerned. "The corner's riding really badly. You're going to have to take the alternative." He didn't look happy. "The Australian girl's just gone clear and into the lead. You'll need a fast clear to shake her off."

Ash passed me my skull cap. My bowels felt as if they were mixing concrete. "I can't do it," I whined. "I can't, I know I can't."

Eric slapped me on the back and by the time I'd spluttered for breath my moment of panic had subsided. This is what I'd decided on, it was either put up or shut up. But it was no use moaning.

Suddenly like a breath of fresh air Jade appeared striding across the grass collecting ring between two six-foot Greek gods, who were sure to be models and had Cam and Zoe swooning.

"I thought I'd offer moral support," she grinned, oozing confidence and happiness. "This is Pete and this is Brian, and they're both on my course."

Zoe's eyes flew up into her eyebrows and I heard her whisper to Cam, "That's it. Forget the physiotherapy, I'm going to be a vet's nurse."

It was a sweet welcome distraction. But then

we had to get down to the start. Barney was prancing sideways and snatching excitedly at the bit. Ash flung me up into the saddle with a leg-up which was more like a fireman's lift, and I tried desperately to stop my teeth chattering. I must look professional. I had to succeed.

Eric was barking instructions, his voice gravelly with tension. "Don't be in two minds or change your plan of attack halfway round. Indecision could cost you the competition."

Jade passed me a four-leaf clover which I shoved down my cross-country shirt. We arrived at the starting area with the largest entourage of support, and it made me feel important and put back some of the shattered confidence. And by the feel of Barney it was doing the same for him.

We popped over a couple of practice fences and waited for our number to be called. There was a buzz of information flying around about the bogey fences and the corner was one of them. I'd take Eric's advice and go for the longer route. Everybody was saying the time was really tight.

"You'll have to fly." Eric tapped my leg. "Foot to the floor all the way round."

I moved towards the starting box. "Good luck!" Jade was waving frantically, Ash smiled and Zoe stuck up both her thumbs. I had the best team of supporters ever.

The starter stepped back as Barney whirled

round, his face deadpan and totally concentrating on the countdown. I pressed my stopwatch. Then I tightened my reins. Barney arched his back in anticipation.

"Three. Two . . ." We blasted forward in an uncontrolled spurt. We were strides away before we were called back. A false start. And valuable seconds ticking away. The clock was still running . . .

I glanced at Eric and his disappointment was obvious. I'd blown it. I'd never make up the time. Ash was mouthing "Don't panic" but I was a wreck. I didn't know what to do next. Barney couldn't understand it and was yanking at my arms, plunging around like a madman. The starter raised his hand for a second time. I circled Barney desperately trying to keep calm.

"Three. Two . . . Wait for it . . . One. *Go!*"

We were away!

I went faster than I'd planned. The first six fences were just a blur. Barney was eating them up like a tiger. I tried to concentrate on the fence ahead, following Eric's advice, looking forward, planning forward. Getting everything right. He was jumping big and powerful and stretching into the bit as we flew down a grassy stretch.

I started to relax and enjoy myself. I was riding with a purpose and it was going to be all right. We were back on form. A hedge, a wall, a palisade, a sleeper on a hill. Ride, ride, ride, check, jump, push on, the wind in my face, the power, the speed; it was all intoxicating.

We were heading towards the corner. It was a difficult approach, coming round a bend and blocked by trees, and then suddenly upon you so you couldn't see a stride. The jump had to be accurate, neither too near the flag to provoke a run-out, nor too much the other side where the V would be at its widest. I'd originally found a good line looking straight ahead and aiming towards an oak tree in the distance. But now there was a mass of trees. I couldn't pick out the right one.

"Be decisive – don't be in two minds." Eric's voice echoed in my head. Barney's ears flicked back waiting for instructions. I decided to go for the direct route. It would save time. I wanted to win.

The corner loomed up, big, solid, three-foot six. I tightened my left rein and pushed my left leg behind the girth to keep him straight. "Come on, Barney, don't let me down." I stroked his neck encouragingly, never taking my eye off the fence.

Three – two – one. I pushed out for the last stride and we rose up in a perfect arch. It was an incredible jump. "If you arrive at a fence well and leave it well, the jump is bound to be good." Eric's words were right with me.

"Good boy." I flung my arms round Barney's

111

neck, letting the reins momentarily drop as I leaned forward.

The next fence was upon us before I knew it. A simple log pile, but at an awkward angle with a bad take-off. Barney was too much on his forehand. He skipped a stride, flattened and skewered over, and somehow my left stirrup flew off as I landed and I fell heavily in the saddle.

"Keep going!" I heard somebody shout from the ropes. I didn't know whether it was Ash or Eric. To have come this far and then for this to happen was unbelievable. I couldn't get my balance. I was all over the place.

"Steady, Barney, whoa!" We jumped the next fence with me getting left behind and very nearly flying over his shoulder.

"Tuck it up, under the saddle flap." Ash was there by the ropes as I steadied to trot to regain my balance.

The penny suddenly dropped. I remembered Mark Todd doing an incredible round with his leg tucked under the saddle flap when the same thing happened to him. I wasn't so tall. I didn't have so far to go.

Barney surged forward, grateful that I was no longer bouncing around. The coffin. Jump, stride, ditch, stride, out again. The pain was excruciating. Mark Todd must have legs like steel pins.

I rode at a simple brush fence. There was

Jade, Zoe and Cam rooting for us like mad, cheering at the tops of their voices.

"Come on, Barney!" I clapped my legs round his sides and we burst into a new gear. We had to make the time. I checked my stopwatch. One minute ten seconds to get home. I closed my eyes and willed my brain to shut out the pain. We were in the frame; we couldn't lose it now.

Fifty seconds.

We were scorching. I'd never ridden at such a blistering pace. Trees and faces just whirred past. I was slipping lower and lower into the saddle.

Thirty seconds. I squeezed harder. As I turned for the last fence everybody was cheering hysterically, delighted at something different. An odd-looking yellow horse jumping like Pegasus and a girl clinging on like a monkey.

Fifteen seconds.

We were over the last and heading for the finish.

"Go on, go on, go on!"

Every stride was an effort. I didn't have to look at my watch. I knew we'd done it. We'd clinched first place.

"Yes!" I punched the air with my fist. We'd done it. We were back on top. I slithered out of the saddle feeling as if my left leg had stretched two foot. It was Barney who was the star. I'd just been a cumbersome passenger. I flung down my crop and hugged his neck with both arms wrapped tight. "I love you, Barney."

People were pushing from all sides. Ash bounded forward and flung his arms round both of us. "And I love you, Alex." His voice was a whisper but it soared in my ears.

"Aren't you the girl who's a model?" Someone pushed forward with an autograph book and pen, staring at me as if I was famous.

"No," I gasped, smiling through tears of happiness. "I've given all that up." I turned back to Barney and kissed his sweaty nose. "I'm a rider through and through."

GLOSSARY

anti-cast roller A stable **roller** which prevents the horse from becoming **cast** in the stable or box.

Badminton One of the world's greatest three-day events, staged each year at Badminton House, Gloucestershire.

to bank When a horse lands on the middle part of an obstacle (e.g. a **table**), it is said to have banked it.

bit The part of the bridle which fits in the mouth of the horse, and to which the reins are attached.

bounce A type of jump consisting of two fences spaced so that as the horse lands from the first, it takes off for the next, with no strides in between.

bridle The leather **tack** attached to the horse's head which helps the rider to control the horse.

cast When a horse is lying down against a wall in a stable or box and is unable to get up, it is said to be cast.

cavaletti   Small wooden practice jump.

chef d'équipe   The person who manages and sometimes captains a team at events.

colic   A sickness of the digestive system. Very dangerous for horses because they cannot be sick.

collected canter   A slow pace with good energy.

crop   A whip.

cross-country   A gallop over rough ground, jumping solid natural fences. One of the three eventing disciplines. (The others are **dressage** and **showjumping**.)

dressage   A discipline in which rider and horse perform a series of movements to show how balanced, controlled, etc. they are.

dun   Horse colour, generally yellow dun. (Also blue dun.)

feed room   Store room for horse food.

forearm   The part of the foreleg between elbow and knee.

girth   The band which goes under the stomach of a horse to hold the **saddle** in place.

Grackle   A type of noseband which stops the

horse opening its mouth wide or crossing its jaw. Barney is wearing one on the cover of *Will to Win*.

hand A hand is 10 cm (4 in) – approximately the width of a man's hand. A horse's height is given in hands.

hard mouth A horse is said to have a hard mouth if it does not respond to the rider's commands through the **reins** and **bit**. It is caused by over-use of the reins and bit: the horse has got used to the pressure and thus ignores it.

head collar A headpiece without a **bit**, used for leading and tying-up.

horsebox A vehicle designed specifically for the transport of horses.

horse trailer A trailer holding one to three horses, designed to be towed by a separate vehicle.

jockey skull A type of riding hat, covered in brightly coloured silks or nylon.

jodhpurs Type of trousers/leggings worn when riding.

lead rope Used for leading a horse. (Also known as a "shank".)

livery Stables where horses are kept at the owners' expense.

loose box A stable or area, where horses can be kept.

manege Enclosure for schooling a horse.

manger Container holding food, often fixed to a stable wall.

martingale Used to regulate a horse's head carriage.

numnah Fabric pad shaped like a saddle and worn underneath one.

one-day event Equestrian competition completed over one day, featuring **dressage, showjumping** and **cross-country.**

one-paced Describes a horse which prefers to move at a certain pace, and is unwilling to speed up or increase its stride.

Palomino A horse with a gold-coloured body and white mane or tail.

Pelham bit A bit with a curb chain and two reins, for use on horses that are hard to stop.

Pony Club International youth organization, founded to encourage young people to ride.

reins Straps used by the rider to make contact with a horse's mouth and control it.

roller Leather or webbing used to keep a rug or blanket in place. Like a belt or girth which goes over the withers and under the stomach.

saddle Item of tack which the rider sits on. Gives security and comfort and assists in controlling the horse.

showjumping A course of coloured jumps that can be knocked down. Shows how careful and controlled horse and rider are.

snaffle bit The simplest type of **bit**.

spread Type of jump involving two uprights at increasing heights.

square halt Position where the horse stands still with each leg level, forming a rectangle.

steeplechasing A horse race with a set number of obstacles including a water jump. Originally a cross-country race from steeple to steeple.

stirrups Shaped metal pieces which hang from the saddle by leather straps and into which riders place their feet.

surcingle A belt or strap used to keep a day or night rug in position. Similar to a **roller,** but without padding.

table A type of jump built literally like a table, with a flat top surface.

tack Horse-related items.

tack room Where **tack** is stored.

take-off The point when a horse lifts its forelegs and springs up to jump.

three-day event A combined training competition, held over three consecutive days. Includes **dressage, cross-country** and **showjumping.** Sometimes includes roads and tracks.

tiger trap A solid fence meeting in a point with a large ditch underneath. Large ones are called elephant traps.

trotting poles Wooden poles placed at intervals on the ground to improve a horse's pacing.

upright A normal single showjumping fence.

Weymouth bit Like a **Pelham bit,** but more severe.